S0-AXV-929

# MORE SHORT ORDERS

*To Ritter, who apparently has no first name! I crafted this little book for your lonely nights in the Subaru.*

*but valuable,*

*Other books by Marty Martindale*

SHORT ORDERS:
Food Stories and Travels
July, 2011

Marty Martindale is owner and
editor of http://www.FoodsiteMagazine.com.

# MORE SHORT ORDERS

*Marty Martindale*
*a.k.a. Margaret Leora Burleigh-Martindale*

Copyright © 2013 Marty Martindale

All rights reserved.

ISBN: 1482589400

ISBN-13: 9781482589405

CreateSpace Independent Publishing Platform

North Charleston, South Carolina

# Short Orders

*Decicated to:*

*My kids, JoAnn and Brad Martindale*

# PREFACE

In this second book following *SHORT ORDERS: Food Stories and Travels*, food is always present as it is in life.

In MORE SHORT ORDERS, Martindale leans more on her concept of the big picture, the big evolutionary picture, through which all people and things progress.

Life is a series of "Short Orders." Very little in life remains as originally conceived. To live happily, we must expect this and affirm this.

Read on!

# MONICA CHERRY WHEN SHE'S NOT TAYLOR JAMES OR LIZ LOVETTI

*Just give me my simple life ...*

Taylor James is her name. She's sixty-six years old and holds double majors in anthropology and political science. How does she spend her days? Taylor James uses the pen name, Monica Cherry, and has, so far, published 126 romance novels about the life and perils of Liz Lovetti, female tormenter and sensual sex goddess. All Monica Cherry's books are torrid, viperous and wickedly lusty, in total contrast to her plain appearance and seemingly somber life.

Monica Cherry has, so far, written 126 novels. She loves titling them. A few of them are:

*Velvet Petals*
*Ancient Lollipops*
*Hellish Raindrops*
*Whispering Worship*
*Saintly Visits*
*Conniving Couples*
*Bogus Begonias*
*Indebted Obstacles*
*Wholloping Whipsticks*
*Bracing Vapors*
*Hit Me, Hit Me*
*Working Joy*
*Vivacious Julieanne*
*Hellish Homestead*
*Evening Mornings*
*Credit Him Evil*
*Vanishing Teardrop*
*Lively Love Talks*
*Heavenly, Heavenly*
*Cake and Caring*
*Honest Deceiver*
*Darling Do Not!*
*Swimsuit Occasion*
*Riviera Rivalry*
*Random Ructions*

And these were only some of many stories Monica had enjoyed weaving.

No matter which hat she wore, Monica Cherry and Taylor James's, only companion was Grover Cleveland. Grover was a handsome, large, Wyoming-bred, four-year-old, steel-gray sheepdog with a loveable hair-strewn face. Twice every day Taylor takes Grover to the park at the end of her block where he sniffs and frolics and she sits on the same bench by a brook and types rapidly on her white minicomputer. Every afternoon, she packed along a canine-safe, chocolate cookie and for Grover, his favorite, and some Belgian, dark chocolate bark laced with caramelized sesame seeds for herself.

At ten in the morning, on the fifth of every month, Groomer Boomer's van picks up Grover Cleveland for his regular grooming. By four in the afternoon, His Nibs returns regal, bushy and laced with essences of Old Spice. Sometimes Boomer turns Grover's facial hair locks into intricate, brightly-beaded braids. Grover was a love!

No car is necessary in Taylor's well-ordered life; everything she needs is delivered: her groceries from Peapod and her drug and general household items from Amazon. Her Barbera wine comes regularly by the case from Milan, Italy, a year-long gift from her lover, Gui. Thankfully, the park at the end of her street hosts farmers on Fridays, where Taylor gets her fresh cherries for good luck, her vegetables, cheese and milk.

Was it because she didn't drive a car or she was never seen talking on a cell phone or because she didn't bother with the styles of the time that made her noticeable? Every day she wore khakis with bright knit shirts all with elbow-length sleeves. She always wore brown sandals, no nail polish, no lipstick, no makeup. Her hair was chestnut brown with bangs to her eyebrows. She carried no purse, only a minicomputer bag strung diagonally across her body. This was Taylor James's happiest way to be.

Truthfully, no one could ever say they had seen Monica Cherry away from home when she was not typing on her white minicomputer, which only added to her mystique. They knew she wrote the Liz Lovetti books, and the only way they could seem near to her was to read her books, which lent a lot of spice to her plainness.

Her publisher's publicist, Sammy Siegel, handles Monica artfully. He has to! In fact, she is his only account—Elite Publishing's cash cow. She refuses all public appearances, but, after years of coaxing, consents to telephone interviews. It took two more years, after Skype came out, for Sammy to trick Monica into appearing visually over her computer's webcam. She did win her own conditions, however. Taylor wasn't at all fussy about how Monica looked, just so long as Monica looked nothing like Taylor. Sammy wisely left her to her own devices, and she came up with a long wig of stringy black hair, very straight. Over it, she chose a red do-rag perched above some very long bangs. She further obscured herself with large, round, black-rimmed glasses.

All interviewers are warned in advance to never ask Monica any personal questions—about where she lives, about her dog or the name of her next book. Despite this, Monica goes into great detail concerning her protagonist, Liz Lovetti, and her fantasy world in Wentworth, California. She especially loves it when a reader asks her why she had Liz do what she did. Monica is never at a loss for an entertaining explanation.

So. What does Monica look forward to, other than each new book?

What sustains her is every year Elite Publishing ships Grover Cleveland express to Nice, France, to be with Monica Cherry as she spends five delicious weeks on the French Riviera at the swank Allier Hotel, which delivers bowls of fresh cherries to her room every morning. There, she wears her interview look, her do-rag, huge glasses and very scant coverings as she cavorts with her publisher-provided lover, Gui. Together she devises a lifestyle for them as if she really were Liz Lovetti. It works!

The rest of the year, Taylor churns out more and more torrid tales of Liz Lovetti. Life is good. Life is predictable. Life is very pleasant for Monica Cherry...until the night Sammy calls her on her land phone. This is unusual, because Sammy never disturbs her evenings.

"Sorry to bother you," he says feelinglessly.

Monica remains silent.

After a short silence, Sammy elatedly says, "I've been talking to Hollywood about you! They love you, Monica."

Monica wishes she was back in her study developing her new character, Ingrid.

"Excelsior Studios wants to make a movie of your *Vivacious Julieanne*! You can write the screen script or let them do it. It's up to you! *Vivacious Julieanne* was always my favorite," Sammy hastens.

Sammy is a damn liar, and Monica knows it. He's never read one of her books. He only makes a living off them.

"I'm not interested," Monica hisses.

"But you gotta be," Sammy returns with angst.

Monica hangs up the land phone with a crashing sound. She hopes she hurt Sammy's ears.

The next few days are a blurred time of unappreciated routine for Monica Cherry. No pack of Hollywood assholes is going to rearrange her work, and she won't help them rearrange it, either. Why couldn't Sammy let things be as they were?

Sammy knows better than to ply Monica with dozens of bouquets of flowers. That is Sammy's trouble with Monica. She is so totally happy with her boring, boring existence.

Sammy stays away from her, and Monica is pleased with this. However, on a Wednesday, near noon, a FedEx Express person comes to her door and hands her a flat box, which she signs for.

The return address is Adrien Ledbetter, Excelsior Studios in California.

"No. They couldn't have!" she screams out loud to no one.

As she feared, inside is a big, fat script with *Vivacious Julieanne* as the working title, adapted for screen by Adrien Ledbetter.

It isn't until the following day, when Monica has cooled off, that she is able to take a look at Adrien's work—her work on Monica's own character!

Monica feels invaded, compromised and awful. She designed her fictional love child, Julieanne, as a genius, yet fragile, gorgeous, yet subdued—they have turned her into a vamp! A vixen! A disaster!

Sammy knows it will be a matter of days before Monica studies the script, if she studies it at all.

On the following Monday, before her first trip to the park, Sammy phones Monica to learn her reaction. Maybe she has softened?

Sammy has to phone three times before Monica answers him, and she does so with silence.

"Monica. I know you find this upsetting. But just think. It will be the grandest pinnacle of your professional life! Couldn't you use a little, really a lot, more money? Maybe live year-round in France, in your own place? Think about it, Monica. I'll call you on Wednesday. Bye."

Better he phone than show up here, she thinks. BUT, there is nothing to think about. Monica goes about her favorite routines, very nearly producing more than average days. Fear, as well as anger, makes Monica work even harder.

This is Grover's grooming week, and he goes off Tuesday to return princely, decked gaily in braids with bright yellow beads. He knows he looks great. Monica thinks so, too.

The next day Sammy calls at exactly ten in the morning.

"Did you read it all? Do you like Adrien's treatment? You know you can write the script yourself; does that appeal to you? Don't just think of yourself, Monica. I stand to benefit from this, too. If you don't take them up on it, I lose, too!

Monica uses silence.

Sammy babbles on, "What if it wins an Emmy? I can see you now on the red carpet. Maybe you'd invite me? Or Gui would come to the US? Say something, will you, Monica?

There is a long silence. Then, in an even voice, Monica speaks her truth.

"Sam, I am sixty-six years old. I am happy. I am happy in what I do. I like my life. Why should I change it? Do you know the value of happiness?"

Silence.

Sammy pressed his "end" button. It was over.

# SEE IT. SOLVE IT.

## Mutual Objectivity

Seasoned travelers, they had circled the world several times. Their plane would leave in an hour, boarding would commence in twenty minutes.

Second-generation, lean-built Asian Americans, they were a guy and gal couple in their late twenties, trimly dressed. Their clothing and backpacks were very REI-travel, in monotones of khaki; their high-grade running shoes, dark gray. He carried a large water bottle they shared; she carried a trail-mix dispenser. Their carry-ons were trim, firm and modest in size.

Their relationship was tight. It was clear they had been together for a long time and were very devoted to one another. They literally fed off of each other's presence.

Their extensive schooling was complete, at least for the present. He was an MIT chemical engineer, she a pharmaceutical microbiologist. Now, for the time being, they were enjoying its rewards with temporary jobs they liked.

As they sat waiting, they leaned slightly against each other, totally patient and very in the moment.

Suddenly he sat up, frowned deeply and withdrew to himself.

Surprised, she sat up too, put her head against his, and they whispered.

He threw his head back, scowled and rolled his eyes. Then, he pushed the right side of his head toward her. He wanted her to look in his ear.

She turned fully toward him and looked gingerly into his ear.

He winced.

She looked even more closely.

He clinched his fists silently.

She scientifically tapped his ear ever so slightly.

He threw his hands up.

She "gentled" his shoulder, then clinically reached into her pocket and retrieved her iPhone.

Neither was talking.

Next, she deftly took a photo of his afflicted ear, once with flash, once without.

They studied the photos minutely, enlarging and collapsing them several times. She seemed to be explaining to him the anatomy of his ear.

They whispered a lot.

He listened intently, his scowl finally waning, his tense shoulders relaxing some, his mouth softening.

He patted his ear gently.

She slid her phone into her pocket.

They assumed a more relaxed position, both for the first time understanding his discomfort.

He checked the clock and drank from their water bottle.

She squeezed his hand and ate some trail mix.

Their boarding commenced.

# OUR ROBOT, CHARLIE

*A review about "SaavyTech" for "Amyzon"*

Want lazy kids? Want an end to the entire icky-sticky, mean, little kitchen jobs you hate to do? Get a robot!

We got Charlie from SavvyTech's Robot Store in our town. Robots come in all sizes and all capacities. Naturally, the greatest advantages in your robot cost more. If you want him sound-free, that costs a whole lot, almost double the price of a stripped-down model. There are grades between

totally silent, tolerably noisy and very damn noisy—
the standard version.

Gender and looks differ. Usually, if a woman plans
to work most with the robot, she chooses a male
name, though males and females are said to possess equal strength and agility. Both genders wear
jeans and T-shirts with their name, which you
choose, and it's printed on your robot's shirt, front
and back. At no extra charge, you get to name
the primary color of your new robot's shirt. Same
for eye color, just so long as you settle for blue
or brown. Robot hair is molded and rigid and another freebie, as long as it is blond or brown. All
of SavvyTech's robots come sans tattoos, jewelry
and bling of any type. All are five feet, two inches
tall. Charlie's, also molded, brown metal shoes are
kind of blended into the base of his jeans; his soles
are pure machinery.

Charlie's feet are like two very large Roombas,
those floor-cleaning disks which go back and forth
on floors. The default for Charlie, when no other activity is programmed, is "Rhoomba-ing" your tiled,
wooden or carpeted flooring. All Charlies are programmed to Roomba from the southwest corner to
the northeast corner of any floor level. When this
is complete, he starts over again. We decided to

keep Charlie on the ground floor, because most of our activity was there and, thus, most of the work.

We can voice-talk to the computer which runs Charlie, or we can type in commands to him. He has his own computer; he is his own omputer. We have two terminals, one upstairs and another on the lower level. It was not easy learning how to *not speak* to Charlie, though I do sometimes. It does no good; he just "heeds" software.

The kids think Charlie's a hoot. Early on we learned we had to stop them from tormenting Charlie. They would go off, hide and giggle as we fussed with our "error in computing."

Charlie has many defaults, just as any good software program does, and we had to learn them. If the computer "in him" crashes, Charlie heads for the armchair at the head of the dining table and drags it into the kitchen and faces it toward the wall. He sits in it, staying very still, until someone comes home and resets his software. Give him a pure command, and the job is just about done. Give him a garbled message, and Charlie merely sits on his haunches and waits for a better command. We had no dinner lots of nights when we first got Charlie, and I guess you can say we were harder to train than Charlie.

Before we received Charlie, I made sure all my recipes and procedures were entered in Charlie's computer. All I do each week is type up a week's menu, bring the groceries and panty items home and put them away. One drawback—if I don't check to be sure we're not going to be out of an item, Charlie emits an evil wail, freezes up and goes into tantrum mode. The alarm goes off, and this holds up all the other foods for the meal, as well. In other words, I am forced to keep a perpetual inventory of all pantry, freezer and refrigerator standard and not-standard items. If we're out of anything at all, dinner's on stall and Charlie's facing the kitchen wall; no heavenly aromas, dinner simply isn't there.

Not to worry: Charlie comes with forty-seven pages of FAQs *before* SavvyTech allows us to ask our own special ones (and SavvyTech checks on this, too!).

One day a month is Charlie's day off. He gets cached. To do this, we carefully lay him onto the floor, on a thick quilt, on his back. Next we open a little door in his foot bottom, remove all the fuzz, kittens and lint from our floors and take a reading of the energy units he's used. This helps calculate our monthly SavvyTech charge for Charlie. On this day, we also spray all of Charlie's joints with lubricant, scrape his intersections for any lint, top off his cleaning-fluid reservoirs, polish his eyes and generally give him a sponge bath with a special SavvyTech robot solution. It makes him shine and keeps him looking great for a few days.

We pay through the nose for virus protection for Charlie. No one's sure if a virus in him might be passed on to us, but we won't afford the risk. SavvyTech charges plenty for this coverage.

Charlie also has a few demands of his own. He won't, or can't, do windows. It's for our protection, too, they told us. It seems Charlie can get so enthusiastic he can break the windows, and SavvyTech has a huge built-in charge to discourage us from deciding to teach this forbidden task to Charlie.

When you spend so much and work so closely with someone who associates themselves so closely with you and your family and he can't talk to you, while you are also in control of his desired emotions—it gets difficult to deal with.

We are also not sure how we feel about Charlie, except we have learned we cannot exist very well without him! Yes. I guess we'd like to express appreciation to Charlie, but how?

We do know this to be true:

When you own a Charlie, you are never right unless you happen to enter data into the computer in its language and it happens to coincide exactly with Charlie's housekeeping goals.

# THE VENABLE, DELICATE BASHFRUIT*

*One If by Day; Another If by Night*

Scientists at a Californian private agricultural institute, in close cooperation with Central American
agronomists, have created a new fruit. Named after
head agronomist, Carl Bash, Bashfruit originated
as a horticultural experiment created first in their
lab, then successfully harvested in nearby fields
six years later. Locals liked Bashfruit instantly.

Bashfruit grows rapidly on very large vines, which
bear big, dark purple blooms and hairy leaves,

similar to squash vines. Underripe Bashfruit are poisonous. Once ripe, the fruit bruises easily, necessitating handpicking and careful crating. This, and the fruit's short, ripe life, accounts for its high cost. Its maximum off-the-vine ripe, edible life is three weeks. This also means it has a very short distribution time.

Bashfruit is rich in fiber, Vitamins *A* and *C* and many minerals.

Bashfruit is unique unto itself for the reason it is sweet by day and savory by night. Any recipe preparation for the sweet, pinkish-yellow Bashfruit must be completed and consumed before sunset; the reverse is true about savory recipes after sunset and its bright purple color. This necessitates careful signage. Cookbooks tend to avoid recipes for Bashfruit due to its time sensitivity.

The Latin name for Bashfruit is: familia of babbeceus fruitae. Its overall size is about ten to twelve inches long and five inches in diameter.

Its pits always number two. They are always separate, both mango-like and flat, with fiberish flesh attached. Each pit is about 2.5 inches by one inch. The

Bashfruit's flesh remains the same in appearance, day and night, a smooth, lightly firm pale green.

Select Bashfruit that is color-appropriate as to time of day, free of blemishes and heavy for its size. Store it in the refrigerator during the day; place it at room temperature during nighttime.

The flesh of the Bashfruit is never cooked. When incorporated into a hot dish, it is folded in after the dish is removed from the heat. The two flavors of Bashfruit are vanilla with a hint of honey by day and, at night, a lemony taste with a hint of sage and cinnamon. Always peel and remove pits. The flesh mashes or cubes well.

SERVING SUGGESTIONS:

Sweet, daytime Bashfruit:

Serve chilled, halved or pitted as cantaloupe.
As a delicate garnish for fruit cup.
In smoothies mixed with strawberries, blueberries and banana.
Chopped in salads, salsas

Savory, evening Bashfruit:

In gravies and dressings
Mixed with vegetables
In stir-fries

Topping for chili

*Note: There is no such fruit as Bashfruit.

# WATER ONE-UPMANSHIP

*What's next?*

Time was when water, with bread, was always served at restaurants.

Then North Americans, who felt flush, started to copy the popular European practice and opted to pay for bottled water; others always received a free glass of tap water.

Then, the States began a water-saving, conservative approach—no water unless requested. Proprietors liked this because it saved manpower money for serving the water, clearing the glasses and having someone else to wash them: It also increased revenue.

Then customers began watching their money more closely and discovered they could order free water to drink with their meal and get the waitstaff to add a slice of lemon to the water and ice—they were swinging! They never did this at home, and here it was free and tasted "kinda" good!

A period of time went by, and it seemed customers had restaurant owners beat. Water became tastier and remained free!

This tale is not over yet. Last week my waitress told me because I ordered an iced tea with my lunch, I was eligible for a free dessert!

Next move?

# A WONDERFUL DAY IN THE PARK

## "It's in the book..."

Owenville is a sleepy, little town and very mindful of what's good for its citizens. In short, it's a good place to live.

Part of this good life is Owenville's new James Owen Memorial Park. It is in the center of town and very green, with an elaborate children's playground, a valley-like band shell with excellent acoustics, a wooded picnic ground with charcoal grills for each table and a free, jolly trolley, which regularly connects the popular park with other busy parts of Owenville.

The jewel of James Owen Memorial Park is the James Owen Cultural Center, resplendent with fountains, hanging gardens and huge, hot-day, ground-level fountains showering frolicking citizens who love jumping and dancing in the water.

The center itself is a double venue, with not one, but two event halls under one roof with common restrooms, a mirrored, lushly-carpeted lobby and a gourmet refreshment center serving in a posh café surrounding another fountain with more hanging gardens.

Inside each concert hall is highly-cushioned, banked seating with rocking-chair comfort—all seats affording unobstructed views of the stage. Separate, high-tech sound systems enhance, as well as insulate, two rock venues in one night. Likewise, the Owen Culture Center's acoustics can protect a soft symphony from a full-fledged rock concert on the same night.

Now, Janet Cole was on the city council and also a member of Owenville's Victory Chapel. And, she was extremely pleased to secure the east theatre of the cultural center, Theatre A, for Sunday afternoon's presentation of Herbert Young, author of *My Good Life is Getting Better*. Everyone in her church loved Young's writings, and this was his latest book! This program was scheduled to begin at two in the afternoon.

Across Owenville, Joy House, a shelter facility for battered women and their children, scheduled their annual picnic celebration at the Owenville Picnic Pavilion to start at noon. They would use the restrooms inside the cultural center. The moms and their kids romped in the playground, took part in relay games and feasted on savory hamburgers and hotdogs cheerfully cooked by the Owenville Lions Club. Most of the feasting was finished by about two fifteen, and, like airplane travelers, small group after small group made their way to the center's facilities. By this time, the Victory Chapel members were closed inside Theatre A, enjoying their favorite author, Herbert Young, discussing *My Good Life is Getting Better*. He would be signing copies of his book afterward in the lobby.

Now, when the moms and their kids arrived to use the facilities, they saw stacks and stacks of Young's enticing book.

"This must be the Lions Club's gift to the women," they thought. Life improvement was always the core theme of their group meetings at the shelter. Word spread quickly. Very soon, family groups, whether they needed the facilities or not, headed up to the center for their free book! How fortunate! Very quickly, the stacks of books were exhausted!

At approximately 3:10, Young invited Victory Chapel's members to follow him out to the lobby where he would sign all purchases. The ushers flung wide the doors; the refreshment center's staff was ready, and parishioners flocked out into the lobby to purchase Young's book and tend personal needs.

They found a flustered Herbert Young with no books to sign.

If the food staff realized what happened, they weren't speaking about it.

However, outside, all the battered mothers were very, very happy.

This had been a wonderful day!

# WIDEWATER PARADISE'S EARLY GLITZ

## *Humble to Glitz to Wrecking Ball*

This is a story about a small, gulfside, illegal gambling roadhouse in the late 1930s, before gambling was legal in Mississippi. In sixty-eight years, the drab, tiny Widewater Paradise went from a drab dive, with little around it, to a posh resort, a failed casino and hurricane washout to a wrecking-ball victim.

Things first looked up for the early roadside property when, in 1958, Carl and Helen Smith, a Texas millionaire and his New Orleans wife, bought the Widewater Paradise. They knew the good life and wanted to bring more of it to the coast. The Widewater would become a first-class hotel, one with hundreds of rooms filling the surrounding acreage plus a large marina. It would draw Jackson's big banking meetings, manufacturers' conferences, annual associations countrywide and be an ideal getaway for all fashionable Southern families. The whole state needed it!

Unfortunately, Carl died soon after the purchase. However, Helen was resolute in going through with their plans. She enlisted two of their nephews to help her conduct her massive project.

First, they greatly enlarged the roadhouse on all sides and added stories to its height. It became the new resort's main building. It was stunning to behold—this new gulfside structure faced with impressive sandstone brick, a circular tumbled pebble drive and an impressive cement-canopy.

The new lobby embraced a huge Henry Beginning blue-glass-foil, mirrored, historical mural across from Carl's life-sized oil portrait.

The new main elevated dining room became the Royal Terrace with a nightly twelve-piece orchestra, flanked by the highly popular Coffee Shoppe, serving three elegant meals per day.

Adjacent to the Royal Terrace was one of four swimming pools, some with submerged, shaded tables for in-pool dining and drinking. These were flanked by the Paradise's Hawaiian-style lanai units.

A dress and lingerie shop in the main lobby, the Helen Smith Shoppe, was "Saturday night close" to the Royal Terrace's continental dining experience and Trophy Lounge.

The Widewater's round Trophy Room had special glass niches in its walls for Mr. Smith's trophies. The house signature drink was the "Winner's Darling," which arrived in its keepsake, shallow sipping bowl of opaque, bright red, and graced with tiny black race horses. It came equipped with a short black swizzle stick topped with a horse's head and a small straw. Horse-head-shaped ice cubes tinkled inside each glass.

Across from the lobby's front desk was a suspended staircase reaching the hotel's mezzanine, site of the administrative offices, switchboard and operation central for Helen Smith and her nephews.

They held forth in a huge drawing-room-sized office with side-by-side desks.

It wasn't long before sizeable conferences and meetings booked the Widewater and poured in from around the country. The hotel instituted a profit-sharing plan for employees, which made us "awfully, awfully nice." Elegant, for the time, meeting rooms had names like Imperial and Empire and were decorated with white marble flooring, accented with lots of royal reds. A rapid-response banquet team lived around town and soon became handy schlepping Green Beans Almandine and Rock Cornish Game Hen onto round banquet tables with skirts they had been taught to pleat themselves.

Every IBM typewriter had a special seahorse symbol key to be struck after each mention of "Widewater Paradise" in all marketing literature and correspondence. This was one of the very many flush resort ideas from the Paradise's prominent Chicago ad agency.

Mrs. Smith loved flowers, so the Widewater had its own greenhouse operated by its own horticulturist, a learned, conscientious fellow who stocked all traffic areas with regal bouquets, centered on all buffet tables and gracing all executives' desks.

An old family friend, a semi-retired male movie star was granted space for a small haberdashery shop, including golfing duds, adjacent to the main building. Attached to it was a tiny photo studio and general hangout for staff photographer. This was not far from the rear of the old roadhouse building, now large and swell, with its brand-new garbage-refrigeration system humming noiselessly along the drive separating it from the expensive executive cottages.

Nothing less than three golf courses were procured or rebuilt by world-famed golf-course designers.

Before long, the hotel boasted 360 rooms in different "districts" across the property, including preserving and creating "executive cottages" out of little "units" behind the old roadhouse. A fleet of golf carts connected the new main lobby building to its new campus of apartment-like wings scattered through the back 260 wooded and landscaped acres.

Chefs were imported from Miami, and the heavily-depended-upon head bellman from New Orleans; the front desk, a local hotel man; a kindly maintenance chief; a career accountant and a hold-over red-headed, nobody's fool, convention manager became the most powerful staff people outside

35

of Helen's operation central. A hard-sell director of sales was imported from New Orleans, and a sweet, little old local lady ran the newsstand between Carl's portrait and the Coffee Shoppe across from the dress shop. It all seemed like a pretend, small town, white-marbled "Hollywood." A weekend here was about as fine as Mississippi life could get, outside of being in New Orleans!

Eventually, Mrs. Smith bought the elegant home next to the property on the west for her second-favorite nephew, L.W., who was the building superintendent of the construction of her $3 million, 150-slip marina across the highway from the Widewater's main building. It boasted boat/hotel room service, heliport, ship-to-shore reservations, the finest boaters' facilities and a hip seafood restaurant. In 1963, this facility was state-of-the-art.

Finally! Finally, the Paradise was complete and, as wanted, *the hotel name* to drop amongst the upper-crust upstate and simply the place everyone, who was anyone, wanted to be seen. Every weekend, they all wanted to be seated at an umbrella-covered, seat-submerged banquette in the Paradise's Lanai pool before primping for a gala night at the Royal Terrace where they would drink, dine and dance the night away surrounded by crisp linens and attentive waitstaff in crisp white jackets.

At first, the handpicked staff and the well-selected locals for lesser positions thoroughly enjoyed their work. Working in a resort, with freebie executive lunch, if warranted, was very nice. The surroundings were like working on a movie set.

Early on, if a waiter ramped down into the kitchen with a tray full of china and happened to smash the tray into the tile floor, broken china bouncing everywhere—this was a cause for great entertainment—a spectacular, leg-slapping occasion. It was nearly two years before every dish in the house was affixed to the wall with its replacement price beside it.

Employee food at the Paradise was very good. Mondays it was delicious (Mississippi maids' wash day menu) Red Beans and Rice, and on Fridays the Seafood Gumbo was unexcelled. They were also generous with executive tab privileges wherein the employee chose from the daily menu. For expedience sake, administrative employees took their lunches in the hallowed, exclusive, closed, Royal Terrace, allowing more room in the Coffee Shop for midday diners.

There were some clouds, however.

The nonconstruction nephew, we called him Big Daddy, held domain over the other desk next to Mrs. Smith. He was in his office most of the time, an extremely eloquent, educated man of the arts with a huge martini problem. He was single then and lived most of the time on the penthouse level, except for a special executive cottage he could use any time he so-desired.

Most of the midlevel help was not present evenings when VIPs with future convention planners were wined, dined, banqueted, gifted, women-supplied, golfed and pampered in every way. However, it did not take long for midlevel employees to learn Big Daddy, when hosting VIPs in the Royal Terrace, had on more than one occasion been seen to be barfing too many martinis onto an attending waiter's tray, then gallantly demanding, "GET ME ANOTHER MARTINI!" On other occasions, Big Daddy was seen by staff through his penthouse's open bedroom door on the morning after, his humongously-ample naked body passed out cold on his bed. Not a morale lifter.

A posh, glitzy atmosphere, delicious food, state-of-the-art equipment and liberal profit-sharing handed-out by an unpredictable hierarchy does not always make for happy employees. The owners did all the right things about profit motive, making the playhouse the envy of others, but they never separated hotel business from their own playtime.

The year was 1964, and the Widewater's perk-lucky employees soon became anxious, and this anxiety manifested itself in a wide variety of ways. It was confusing to work hard pleasing strangers in order to please their "boss," when their boss barfed for them and gave other disillusioning displays. It got to where the horticulturist moved a sleeping cot into the greenhouse, so he could all-too-anxiously watch over his flowers. The little old lady in the newsstand's arthritis became disabling. The accountant developed a serious thyroid malfunction. The amiable maintenance super kept circling a certain storeroom, extremely anxious about a fire that wasn't there. The sales secretary went into a deep funk of a depression and quit.

There was something very disconcerting about doing your best on a job and having management disable the result. Just as guests need pampering, employees need a sense of approved accomplishment, and when denied, they suffer.

The ultimate demise of the Widewater Paradise came as no surprise as it dwindled from a top resort to a failed, legal casino, then was devastated by a hurricane and finally put under the wrecking ball.

# EVERYBODY GIVES MORE WHEN THEY RECEIVE SOMETHING

*"I get the best treatment!"*

Mary rushed into Dr. James's office and signed in. She was late.

"I just finished baking my famous 'Better-than-Sex Quadruple-Chocolate Brownies,'" she gushed and giggled to the staff inside the glass window.

All the women working behind the glass smiled obediently.

Mary squeezed into a single chair between two men, her precious parcel of chocolate treats balancing carefully on her knees.

Drs. Russ James and Jim Thorpe had been in practice together for eleven years. Their moderately large waiting room had wooden armchairs around most of the four walls, except for the office window and adjacent door where the nurses welcomed patients back into the doctors' offices.

Most were reading or sitting quietly, then…

"Are you expecting better care than I get with the food you bring?" the distinguished gentleman to her right asked rather casually.

Mary, a little nonplused, replied, "Well, no. It's just that I know they all like my special brownies. I bake brownies for them every time I come here."

"So, this ensures you superior care every time? he prodded.

"No," Mary responded defensively. "I just do it because it makes me feel good."
"So, you do the baking for yourself, instead?"

"They eat them," Mary assured lamely. "I don't."

"Is that really the point?" the gentleman pushed even further.

"Look," Mary stated as she raised her voice, "I was so busy waiting for them to finish baking, it made me late, and I had to rush."

"Do you think our doctor and his staff would be more grateful if you were on time and brought no brownies?"

Mary sat stunned and flushed. Who was this man? Why was he doing this to her?

Neither patient knew the doctors and their staff had solved this problem long ago: first, they rejected the idea of a waiting room sign such as, "PLEASE DON'T FEED THE DOCTORS," and finally opted for a unanimous, in-house policy:

"Trash all foods from outside sources."

# CAPTAIN NO MORE

## *Realizing life does have details*

Fred lived up near DC, where he was raised before he sailed most of the seven seas. Now, semi-retired, age sixty-two, he kept a camper trailer in Florida where he particularly enjoyed a local spiritual church, tanning his naturally-bronzed skin on its beaches and, quite frequently, seeing me after church for an afternoon at the beach and a snack somewhere before day's end.

The new-age church was one for a lot of singles, thoughtful people, no one oozing doctrine at one another. In fact, most came from their own artistic space, and the anonymity of each was respected. Fred, for instance, was very into Ram Dass.

Away from church, Fred was proud of his association with the sea and proud of being half Italian, thanks to his mom. Though in his sixties, he was still trim, his skin a flawless olive tone; he did a lot for a Speedo, and he almost always wore his well-seasoned, squashed captain's hat and equally well-worn Birkenstock classics.

The more I got to know Fred, the more I realized what a highly responsible job being a ship captain is. The whole vessel and everyone aboard is his sole responsibility, no matter how bad the seas. Unfortunately, there's a downside to captaincy work: demon alcohol!

"They seemed great, all those years of partying," Fred recalled solemnly. "One of my perks was to ask, 'Who's fucking the captain tonight? I was always king of the roost!'" By the time I met Fred, his boozing, partying and responsibilities for weighty decision-making had taken a toll on him. He had been sober for ten years and seemed tragic about it, looking forward to his AA meetings on a regular basis.

The son of an American medical doctor and an Italian exchange student, Fred had an easy early life. After his father died, he remained close to his mom, who taught him how to cook and appreciate his Italian heritage. Fred was also his own person. Besides his hat and Birks, in true captain fashion, Fred always had a black valise, which may have been his dad's, the type doctors carried when they made house visits. It was large, made of black leather, hinged and opened at the top. The captain in him made sure it contained a change of clothes, water, a book and a few tools. The Fred in him made sure it contained something to eat, some water and, on at least one occasion, a full-fledged picnic banquet!

Even in his little Florida trailer, Fred cooked for himself, any fancy dish he was in the mood for. One Sunday in particular, he mumbled something about some mesquite and something he wanted me to try. I let it unfold. After we'd sunned for a couple of hours, he suggested we move back to the trees and get one of the picnic tables.

He opened the black bag and lifted aside some cold packs. Next he lifted out two crisp, white table napkins, and another he spread in the middle of the table. Next was a large foil-wrapped package which he placed on the silver plate in the middle of the table. This was followed by a covered, closed container and some loosely-wrapped lettuce.

"There's more, but let's get this open," he urged.

The large foil pack revealed two plump, perfectly-roasted squabs, golden-brown and juicy.

"I had to wait until I found some non-commercial mesquite wood," he confessed.

Over the next container, he said, "These are some fresh fava beans I cooked and marinated in olive oil and spices. They're good!"

The lettuce turned out to be velvety Boston lettuce. "I thought we'd eat the squab wrapped in lettuce," he announced. "I have spoons somewhere for the beans. And, here are a couple of silver crab forks in case we want to scavenge the carcasses."

Next he unloaded some fresh Italian Monte Veronese cheese and a very crusty, skinny loaf of Italian bread. "For dessert, I made a little Capri cake, dark chocolate with almond flour—my mother's recipe," he explained.

Before closing his bag, Fred removed a bottle of imported Italian, non-alcoholic beer for him and a bottle of imported Italian Barbera wine for me.

A light breeze blew in off the water, and we feasted on Fred's mellow, smoky, tender squab morsels with bites of crusty bread dipped into the fava bean herb oil, herbed with oregano and cardamom. We sipped and picked slowly—and slowly picked some more—savoring every bite, inspired by its combination with the next bite of something different. Fred had the touch. He knew it, and the treat was mine!

The food mostly gone, the right amount of wine remaining, we knew dessert wouldn't taste right until we waited for a time—good company and excellently-prepared food on a beautiful beach day—life was good.

I always enjoyed Sunday afternoons with Fred. We didn't meet weekly, and a couple of weeks later, he asked me to drive him north to a town where he had contracted to take a sailing ship replica across the Gulf of Mexico to Progresso, Mexico. It took several trips to the ship before the voyage began. Fred, as captain, could reject any aspect of the ship's condition, provisions or outfitting until he was satisfied it could safely make the trip to Progresso.

It was on the fifth day, his black valise packed to go each day, he determined the ship seaworthy. It was getting dark as the ship left its berth and I pulled away into the dusk. Last I looked at the departing ship, two large barn owls—not a common sight—flew skyward from the nearby mangrove.

I never saw Fred again. It wasn't until recently I read an obituary stating he had passed.

# CHARCUTERIE CAPER

*"May I help you, ma'am?"*

The formal name is "charcuterie." However, most everyone calls it "the deli." Here, impatient customers get their regular nitrate fix, a substance the body doesn't like; but, like smoking, they are indifferent. The stuff is also expensive, and the poorest customers tend to buy the most.

Something seems to take control of charcuterie customers as they wait. Even the humblest of them tend to almost command their dedicated deli worker to produce this, slice this, "let me see if it's thick enough," or "thin enough," finally granting a reluctant go-ahead. It seems they gain a sense of power while exercising this control.

On this particular day, Woody was working the counter alone. He had been carefully slicing and doling out "trates" for twenty-seven years, his right arm visibly larger than his left. He had learned many years earlier to psych himself up to seem as if he thrived on excessive "do thises," and "do thats." Always smiling, he would remind himself the day always passes.

On the other side of the counter, Elsie grabbed her deli customer number and waited for Woody to call it. It was an encouraging three numbers away.

The short time dragged slowly as she mentally rehearsed her order.

"Twenty-six," Woody called. It was Elsie's number.

"I want some Serrano ham, and slice it rather thick." She used her right index finger and thumb to demonstrate.

Woody nodded as he carefully retrieved a previously opened, carefully re-closed Spanish ham and carefully unwrapped it again. He slung it up onto the slicing table, set it for semithick and rolled a first slice. He dutifully placed the slice onto paper and handed it to Elsie for her to taste.

Elsie liked it. "Give me an eighth of a pound; will you please?"

Woody obediently cut the few thick slices, wrapped them and asked if there'd be anything else.

"Give me a little souse," she responded. "Cut it medium."

Woody repeated his seek, unwrap, hoist, slice and hand-first-slice-to-customer ritual.

"It's delicious. And that's a good thickness, a quarter pound, please," she added.

This done, the souse returned, Woody asked about more.

"I want some Genoa salami, the imported, cut it medium, too."

Woody performed his ritual once more; Elsie, enjoying the labor-intensity of it all, announced as he was finishing, "I also want some boiled ham. Slice it medium again. Make it a half-pound.

Woody steadily performed his drill.

Elsie then had him repeat it all and her samples for small amounts of Corned Beef, Bologna, Swiss cheese and Cotto Ham.

Woody did this all day long. It didn't matter for how many people.

"OK," Elsie announced. One more thing. "I'll take a pound of your white Cheddar."

"A full pound?" Woody asked.

"Yes, a full pound of white cheddar, and slice it paper-thin for me."

Elsie approved her sample and nodded for him to start slicing.

Woody turned, went back to the slicing machine and slowly, one by one, stacked and separated a tall pile of paper-thin slices of white cheddar.

During his cheddar stacking, Elsie turned, left the charcuterie, walked empty-handed past the checkouts and into the market's sun-drenched parking lot.

It had been a delicious, excellent lunch…

# BULLY REVISITED

## *Degrees of Separation*

Returning to Providence, Rhode Island, after a fifty-year absence, for an IACP annual meeting, was fascinating. I was impressed by the good retired people there who, hard hit by a poor economy, displayed such pride in their convention center. They enthusiastically volunteered for whatever it took to pull off successful meetings there.

I was to learn one of the liveliest workers, Sam, was also active at a large church I used to attend as an elementary-school child. He was so eager to please I even prevailed upon him to call an old boyfriend for me and see if we could meet. He was pleased to oblige.

Sam also asked me if I'd like to visit our mutual church. Travelers Aid had Sundays off, so he and his sister always volunteered to make sandwiches there for the homeless downtown before church began. They would pick me up at my hotel after the sandwich making.

The church had been a rare Protestant cathedral in a medium-sized city of many large churches. When I was a kid, the large, cross-shaped, domed church attracted an affluent congregation, and adult members of the choir and Sunday school teachers were paid! I sang, unpaid, in their youth choir. We practiced twice a week and performed once a month, without sheet music, robed in purple velvet with white surplices.

The church looked smaller, as is always the case for returning adults. It showed its age, and the congregation was no longer affluent. So many years later, I found a female pastor assisted by a John Lennon-type hippie, whose wife was absent because she was active in another denomination. To my chagrin, I was introduced to the entire congregation as someone from Florida who was attending the food meeting where Sam was volunteering that week. Afterward we went back to the fellowship hall, and I ran into the daughter of my mother's girlfriend, who crooned, "Your mother always liked us to save our ham bones for your pea soup!"

I felt she wanted me to bark, pant and maybe stand on my hind legs.

Earlier, Sam's sister, Ann, said she'd love to drive me around to my old neighborhoods, if I liked, and we could have lunch at the Old Grist Mill, which had been a favorite of mine. I always liked the Johnny Cakes they served everyone. This trip, two new menu items were interesting—their Grilled Littlenecks and Lobster Stuffed with Additional Lobster.

After we lunched, Ann took me by the home where *Providence*, the TV series, was filmed.

During our day's sojourn I recalled event after event as we passed places familiar to me. I even remembered how snobby the rich choir kids, all in private schools, were to the public-school-me.

"One girl in particular," I recalled, "her name was Ann Jones. She was tall and had flaming red hair. Every school day we practiced, she'd ask me if I forgot to wear my school uniform. Of course, I had none, and she knew she succeeded in making me feel foolish."

The reminiscing day was over all too soon. My hostess dropped me off at my hotel and went home to her little cottage and her cat. She had been widowed for many years and met her brother for early-morning walks each day. We hugged, enthused over all the good things we did and bid farewell.

Reflections can come after the fact. It was easily a year later when it became vividly clear to me that the once-redheaded, tall choir bully had been my snow-white-haired hostess that Sunday as we drove to my familiar places.

So many years later, so humble, willing and so serving, she had willingly acted as the food writer's chauffeur while I unconsciously had no problem recounting her unkind actions many years earlier.

I will always wonder if she realized she was the redhead I had was innocently referring to…did she realize I was the public school kid she bullied?

# EXTREME ECOSYSTEM

*Warm, Dark and Tasty*

Edith Jones was a very happy person, easy with a laugh, quick to help others and generally, all-around curious. She also loved life and wanted everyone else to. Whenever anyone suggested a movie, a Tupperware party, a walk on the beach or just coffee anywhere, Edith was there. She had been unemployed for so long that she "no longer looked" as the labor reports said. Anyhow. Life was too much fun this way.

One of Edith's signatures was her large, imposing black plastic, patent-leather handbag. The black plastic was all bunched up against a chipped brass opening with a clasp. In it, she carried lipstick, her wallet, a book to read, a fresh T-shirt in case she slobbered on herself, some wipes, pens, a small pad of paper, some TUMS, a small bottle of aspirin, a proxy brush, a hair brush, eyeliner, mascara, tweezers, a flashlight, some flip-flops, her IDs, a good-luck pom-pom her friend Harriet had given her and some Kleenex.

Because Edith was on the go so much, she never took the time to eat as she should, so this meant stopping in at convenience stores for little somethings to tide her over. She never ate a lot at one time but consumed tiny snacks all day long. This meant there was a goodly number of snacks and partial snacks also in Edith's large black, oversized patent leather purse. On this particular day, she had most of a Baby Ruth candy bar, some red licorice her grandson had shared with her, two peanut butter cups, some crumbled peanut butter crackers, a fresh package of jerky, half a carton of Kozy Shack pudding, a whole banana, the end of a Snickers bar and some Dentyne gum. The floor of Edith's handbag was matted down with wrappers, red gummy bears and worms and crumbled crackers. The more food she had on hand, the more secure it made her feel.

This was not all that was in Edith's go-everywhere, super-sized black patent-leather purse. She also had small colonies of American cockroaches and German cockroaches. These dwelt amongst a troop of small black ants, in-and-out fruit flies and slow-moving maggots. They abided and gnawed in the warm, dark and tasty confines of Edith's generous handbag.

This meant Edith was no stranger to bugbites. Sometimes she withdrew a hand with blood on it. Her critter world didn't like her plowing through her treasures. Their territories were colliding!

"Yes," Edith mused, "I'll have to go through my bag one of these days. I know I have some marshmallows in there, somewhere. I just can't find them."

Now. Everything wasn't all snacking, getting around and visiting for Edith. Whenever she went to visit her sister, Alice, her husband, Charlie, made her leave her purse in the mudroom.

"That damn thing's got roaches, Edith. I don't want it in this house!" ranted Charlie.

"That's my handbag. I like it with me," Edith responded. "I don't know anything about roaches.

What makes him think that," she muttered to herself.

Some days, when Edith walked to her bus stop, a large, black pit bull would run up to Edith, barking and licking her black patent-leather handbag. He slobbered all over her purse, and Edith didn't like it. What could she do?

Usually, the bus would turn the bend, and quickly Edith escaped the looming dog.

On a more recent day, the scene was different when an old woman Edith didn't know attempted to send the dog away from Edith, and quickly the pit bull bit the old lady's hand rather ferociously.

Edith's bus came and went without her. The little woman writhed in pain on a nearby bench. The dog had scampered away. Edith attempted to put her arm around the old woman, but she pushed her off.

This prompted a man from inside the house by the bench to come out and tell the old woman, "I'll go to court with you and testify. This woman carries food or something in her purse every time she walks by here, and she always attracts that menacing dog, and he's dangerous!"

All Edith wanted to do was visit, do good and enjoy a snack now and then. Now what?

Edith's court date came all too soon, and she found herself being sentenced for wanting to visit, do good and snack now and then.

The judge listened carefully first to the old woman, then the man and finally Edith.

At sentencing time, the judge called Edith to come forward.

"I am not going to sentence you to any time nor am I going to suggest any house confinement. You will remain free. I am, however, going to order you to carry no purse for a period of sixty days. This means both of your hands will be free. You will carry all you need in your pockets. Do you think you can do this?"

Edith tried to imagine herself on the bus without a handbag. She would feel naked!

"I will try, sir," Edith murmured. And so she did.

# FABRIZIO'S FAMILY FEAST

## *Native Italians Doing what Native Italians do Best*

There is a beautiful part of the world known as the Piedmont region and Italian/French Riviera bordering the Ligurian Sea on the north of Italy.

Along this privileged area a little south of the Ligurian Alps are the towns of Genoa, Italy, and to the west, Monaco, France. Midway is the terraced, quaint little town of Ormea; its walls are neatly constructed from hand-hewn, layered stone snuggled into the lush, forest-covered mountains dotted with stone walls intersected by meandering streams.

These come together around old homes, seventeenth-century churches, chestnut drying sheds, community ovens and necessary water channels. This is a land of abundant boar, deer, golden eagles and wild trout. This is also where wild, fragrant lavender and exotic Martagon lilies flourish.

Living here are contented people preparing tempting dishes from garden vegetables, herbs, local olives, capers, chili peppers and anchovies against backdrops of quality, local extra-virgin olive oil and locally-unique pastas. They also use a lot of local mushrooms, corn flour, buckwheat, barley and local pecorino and raschera cheeses in their cooking.

My favorite chef, Fabrizio Schenardi, was born in this Piedmont region of northwestern Italy and received his formal culinary education in Switzerland. His family is very food—very, very food. His wife is a chef; his mother a retired baker and his father an olive grower. His aunt was a top chef in San Remo and her daughter a teacher at the Culinary Institute of Arma di Tagglia. His cousin, Giuseppe, was the chef at the Savoy in London.

So, when this food family cooks for themselves, they fix foods they treasure, dishes like their Bagna Cauda of baked, garlic-infused olive oil with anchovies atop a bell pepper topped with mascarpone and served with potatoes. Other dishes they like are fresh-caught hare cooked with raisins, wine fume blanc and cream or a concoction called Finanziera alla Piemontese, which is rooster face parts combined with cornichons, wine, truffles and mushrooms. They smoke their own jerky for two weeks and also stuff animal stomachs with mixtures of chestnuts, hazelnuts, pine nuts, pork blood and leeks. They like their beef with anchovies, their guinea hen breaded with brandy and pumpkin braised with porcini mushrooms with grappa in puffed pastry. So too, fava beans with fish in an herbed tomato sauce, also black figs with rosemary, slowly roasted in port and finished with blue cheese. A favorite dessert is a creation from chestnut flour, raisins, pine nuts and mascarpone.

So in 2009, when Fabrizio, who has been the executive chef for several US resorts from Hawaii to California to Tampa to St. Louis, visited with his family in the Piedmont, he was very happy when they wanted to go as a group for a meal at Cagna da Beppe restaurant, located near Ormea in the province of Cuneo.

The restaurant is located in the middle of the mountains and has an attached hotel, which has been owned by the same family since the 1800s. They specialize in local foods in an idyllic setting, which fronts the trout-filled Tarano River in the middle of the area's lush pristineness. Their bread comes from the bakery next door, where it's baked in a brick oven over chestnut wood. Some of their popular offerings are leek pie, tuna pate, chestnut dumplings, corn-flour pastas, scrupulously-cleaned Ligurian snails and rabbit in white wine with sweet chestnuts, usually served with local wines.

This is what the family ordered and feasted upon as Fabrizio relates:

"First, we start with snails, escargot in their shells. They have been cleaned for one week then sauteed with garlic and olive oil and deglazed with fresh crushed tomato, chopped parsley and basil. They always serve them in a terra-cotta pan with bread from Triora."

The family ate slowly and thoughtfully.

Next, they agreed upon ordering the Gnocchi Alle Ortiche. "This is classic potato gnocchi but with fresh, young nettles added. They serve it tossed with creamy Castelmagno cheese from nearby Cuneo."

Then followed Pansotti, a local ravioli stuffed with marjoram, herbs, ricotta, eggs and fresh Parmesan. They serve it with a walnut sauce.

"Our big dish was their Tajarin al Cinghiale. It is tagliatelle with Parmesan cheese with wild boar, which has been braised in red wine with juniper berries and dried porcini mushrooms." They also ordered Corzetti as a side.

They spent a long time enjoying, telling how they liked to fix the dish and talking about family. The memorable day was dwindling, the sun wanting to disappear behind the mountains, with just enough time for dessert.

"We ordered the Semifreddo al Barolo Pigato," Fabrizio recalls. "It's a traditional semifreddo with a reduction of Barolo and Pigato wines served with Pasta Frolla Biscotti and grape Marmalade. Delicious!"

"It was a beautiful day," Fabrizio smiles.

# FAQ'S—SO THEY KNOW YOU

*You ask the nicest questions.*

Candy Adkins is a lively girl, bright, too. Now twenty-four, she is single, fun-loving and a popular friend.

Candy is applying for a new job. It is for Future's Wholesale Pasta Products. She was never sure what she wanted to do for a career for herself. She had been working as a restaurant hostess while she was attending the local community college. She just completed her AA, and she wasn't sure what she wanted to do. If she remained in school, she would need to pick a major. If she worked instead, she'd have to try and convince someone her basic associate of arts suited her for something. She also had to quit hostessing!

Candy looked very nice at her interview with Edward Futures, the personnel manager. Ed was impressed with Candy as they seated themselves in his office. The room was quiet as he looked carefully at her resume and studied even more closely the company's questionnaire she had completed.

"Nice. One problem. What do you want to do for us, if we hire you?"

"I don't know what you need," Candy replied.

James moved on. "What did you like best in school? English? Social science?"

"I liked creative writing."

"That's fine. But, I can't tell from this what you do best. Tell me. Do you believe you do the best work when it is something you are interested in?" Futures asked.

"I do."

"I don't see where you attached our FAQs."

"FAQs? I forgot them."

"You should know that NO EMPLOYER accepts 'I forgot' when work is incomplete."

Candy flushed. "Yes, sir."

"These tell us a lot. They are thirty questions you compose; then you also compose the answers, keeping in mind what you think is part of a good plan for Future's Pasta."

"I will work on it."

"Tell you what. I will give you another chance. Make an appointment to come back with them."

Candy returned to Futures's office the following Wednesday, Futures's FAQs and answers in hand.

He deliberately had her handwrite her questions and answers, because he wanted to know how well she wrote and, further, was she adept at reading her own writing. Could she read with conviction?

Futures silently studied the three sheets Candy had written.

Candy felt like he was taking a very long time.

Futures handed Candy back her FAQs and bid her to read them aloud.

This is what Candy read: (Her answers were limited to brief responses.)

*Do you wish you were older or younger?*
*Neither.*

*What do you call your father?*
*Dad.*

*What is your biggest talent?*
*Writing.*

*What are you the worst at?*
*Dancing.*

*Second biggest talent?*
*Organization.*

*What are you smartest at?*
*Understanding behavior.*

*If you are in charge of a storage area, is it "the area" or "my area" ?*
*The area.*

*Why would you eat less white flour and high-fructose syrup?*
*To keep weight down and avoid diabetes.*

*If you cook butter, flour and milk together, what are you making?*
*White sauce.*

*What is your favorite color?*
*Taupe.*

*What is your favorite unpopular food?*
*Anchovies.*

*Is work good? Why?*
*Yes. It makes fun more fun.*

*Are vacations good? Why?*
*Yes. They are a change from work and a chance to travel.*

*You are at lunch with clients and you spill a lot of food on your shirt. What do you do?*
*Excuse myself, wash it off in restroom and return.*

*A client complains about the company to you. What do you do?*
*Listen. Relay to company.*

*A client gives you a personal compliment. What do you do?*
*Thank them and modestly tell company.*

*A client compliments the company. What do you do?*
*Thank them and write it up for the company.*

*Would you like to be president of this company?*
*No. Enjoy behind the scenes more.*

*Do you think Future's Pasta Products should be larger?*
*Only if they can make a profit and increase their number of products.*

*What do you think about large families?*
*The world is too crowded for large families.*

*How old is too old?*
*When good health has gone.*

*Would you enjoy military service?*
*No. I don't like violence.*

*What sport makes the most sense to you?*
*I like the penalty box in hockey. I don't like its roughness.*

*Do you participate in any sports?*
*No.*

*What is your favorite type of night out?*
*Dinner, good wine and conversation.*

*Briefly, how is pasta made?*
*Mix flour, egg and water.*

*What is your favorite pasta dish?*
*I like carbonara.*

*Are supervisors smart?*
*That's why they are supervisors.*

*Which of two important tasks would you work on first?*
*The one with the earliest deadline.*

*Do you use recipes on product boxes? Websites?*
*Yes.*

*What will the future hold for food, your worldview?*
*I think someday there will be no ethnic foods. Everyone will eat "World."*

Candy handed the FAQs back to Futures when she had finished reading.

Futures sat looking thoughtfully across the room, a bit of a frown on his forehead.

"Would you enjoy the pasta business?" Futures asked.

"I want to learn some business, and I like working with food," Candy responded.

"Tell you what," he said. "We will try you for one month. During this time we can see how you like it here and how we think you will fit into Future's Wholesale Pasta."

Candy looked a little surprised and pleased.

Futures went on. "Let me ask you a question."

"OK," she agreed.

"Which response do you think impressed me the most?"

"The one about knowing how pasta is made?" she asked.

"No," Futures responded. "I am especially interested in your worldview of food, where you said you think ethnic will be erased in the future. I happen to agree with you. Too many people have a worldview of nothing. Right now pasta is riding quite high, bolstered by the demand for noodles in Asian food."

Candy nodded.

"We will see this change," he promised.

# WHAT EVER HAPPENED TO SUNDAY BRINTHROPE

## *"Our Gal Sunday" Spoof*

*Once again, we present Our Gal Sunday,*
*the story of an orphan girl named Sunday*
*from the little mining town of Silver Creek, Colorado*
*who in young womanhood married*
*England's richest, most handsome lord, Lord Henry Brinthrope.*
*The story that asks the question:*
*can this girl from the little mining town in the West*

*find happiness as the wife of a wealthy and titled Englishman?*

Every weekday, five days a week for twenty-five years, the living rooms all over North America filled with the above question, and millions of fans listened intently to the unfolding tale of a small, abandoned baby girl. Two grizzly miners found her, by chance, next to the silver mine in Colorado where they worked. They named her Sunday, for they found her on a Sunday.

The little girl's childhood was far from a plentiful one. It was rather one of lack and just enough food to get by. She spent a good deal of her growing years playing with no other children but in pubs where her guardians drank regularly with their friends.

The sun does manage to shine down on even the lowliest, and so it was that English-born-and-bred Lord Henry Brinthrope looked in on his silver holdings in far-away Colorado one day, spotted the grown Sunday nearby and had to have her for his own. He promptly whisked her away from the grizzlies to a complicated life at Black Swan Hall in the stately part of Virginia's mountains.

As the years rolled on, she painstakingly learned the ways of grace and plentitude, dutifully taking on the privileges of wealth. For the soap opera's sake, the twenty-five years were filled largely with sagas of North American single women who felt they were a better mate for Sir Henry, and they set to knocking Sunday off her delicate pedestal. Again, in more soap opera tradition, Sunday would always triumph and remained Lady Brinthrope and Lord Henry's everlasting love.

If we were asked to surmise what happened to the couple after their radio tales ended, we come up with this:

Sunday and Lord Henry spent their summers back in the UK while Henry attended his sickly, widowed mother. When they did get away, she was aghast to learn Henry adored spending time in pubs! How, too vividly, Sunday remembered the dingy bars back in Colorado and how her two caretakers would take her to them, drink their beer with their buddies and tell very rough stories.

"English pubs are different," Henry defended. "For one thing, pubs are well known for serving good, home-cooked food." Then, he'd hastily order the pub's "du jour."

But, alas! Males, rich or poor, have a way of predeceasing their wives. This left the poor, mining-town waif alone in her new glittering world, saddled with Lord Henry's millions and a huge Virginia home. What was a new widow to do? She could not return to Colorado!

After a time, Sunday felt she could combine her sense of the past with a part of Lord Henry's English life. She would convert Black Swan Hall into a destination SQUEAK BANGER PUB! Sunday designed it to compliment the Hall's lofty location in the lush, memorable green hills of Henry's "Ole Virginny." Henry loved his Bubble and Squeak, one of the few dishes Sunday would invade the Black Swan Hall's kitchen to make for him when he was alive.

Sunday spared little of Lord Henry's millions to redesign the new Black Swan Hall. The foyer had a hat-check area and seven Bubble and Squeak game machines. Over the doorway to the inner great room Sunday hung this sign:

Welcome to the Squeak Banger Pub:

What mortals Bubble call and Squeak,
When midst the Frying-pan in accents savage,

The Beef so surly quarrels with the Cabbage.

*Peter Pindar Wolcott (1738-1819)*

Inside, a huge mahogany bar was built, and it ran in a horseshoe loop for four hundred feet. Surrounding it were scores of heavy, plank-like tables with stout chairs. The walls were silhouetted in black to simulate the city of London. In the foreground, artists painted quaint pubs with three-dimensional shingles swinging from each.

On the pub's largest wall was nothing but a huge, painted, black board with bold gold lettering of the pub's everyday menu, one Lord Brinthrope might have suggested himself:

Deer Bangers and Sweet Mash
Brussels's Sprout Bubble and Squeak
Sweet Potato Cottage Pie
Goat Blood Pudding with Goat Cheese Sauce
Haggis stuffed with Sage Sausage
Lamb & Tabasco Hotpot
Eel and Mashed Pie
Panackelty with Corned Beef and Parsnips
Ploughmen with Prosciutto and Farm Cheese

Pork Pie with Apples and Sauerkraut
Chorizo Shepherd's Pie
Lamb and Carrot Scouse
Toad in Yorkshire Hole
Welsh Rarebit, Grilled Cheese smothered with Cheese Sauce

SIDES OF:
Pickled Eggs
Pickled Cockles
Cornish Pasty
Pork Scratchings

FREE DESSERT:
Spotted Dick with Dried Plums

Sunday, herself, greeted and dismissed every pub guest, assuring them, "Henry and I look forward to your swift return."

The pub made Sunday her second fortune.

# THE SHAKE 'N' SPEAR

*Home of Ghouly-Ghouly Sauce*

Mahboo was not a sophisticated, sun-drenched Pacific island. It was far from the States, quiet, just local people, except for Jim, and that was the way they liked it. The islanders took to Jim immediately after he returned following the war. He decided to stay forever. He married a local girl, Tessie. That was ten years ago; they had no children and liked it that way. This meant they could sit on the beach for hours, not talking, and literally feast on its beauty and each other's company.

The couple's only source of income, and they didn't need much, was their little shanty eating place open for business at their convenience. It never lacked for business, however. It was very relaxed, and everyone on the island, it seemed, came to eat their famed Shake 'n' Spear, the only food Jim and his wife served, other than ale or lager.

Together, Jim and Tessie designed the simple menu. Jim wanted it to have a little style but a much-understated style. This is why, several years back, he whittled some slender bamboo into two-pronged spears for his Shake. He'd fashioned them as he and his new love sat by the surf.

Tessie would smile endlessly at Jim, her dimples deep, eyes twinkling.

Jim would say, "You're the most gorgeous woman in the world!"

Tessie would throw her head back and shake her boobs at him.

Jim loved it.

Their Shake came in three varieties: Turtle meat, fish and vegetable. There were several species of turtles in the area, large ones, and Tessie had a secret island way of marinating them. She also had secrets for preparing uniform chunks of twenty-seven varieties of fresh-caught fish. Jim rounded up fresh root vegetables at the island open market, and Tessie marinated these, too, before she parboiled them and Jim dipped them into Tess's breading mixture then fried them.

They had a lot of fun with the preparation. Tessie ground and grated and crushed all manner of dry items and spices to arrive at her magic breading. She never told Jim what was in it, and he never asked. Nor, did Tessie ask Jim what he dipped the food pieces in before shaking them vigorously in her dry mixture.

The cooked result was the tastiest, crunchiest, goldenest-brown nuggets the islanders had ever enjoyed. Even the fat Jim used for frying was a mystery to Tessie. She knew he started with coconut oil, but he did lots of things to it before he heated it and plunked the magic battered morsels in.

Everyone who dined at Shake 'n' Spear received a coconut-husk bowl filled with Jim's Shake, another bowl half-filled with Tessie's Hot Ghouly-Ghouly Sauce and one of Jim's personally-honed bamboo spears.

"GG Sauce" was so hot every native had to work up a tolerance for it, and even more of a secret than Tessie's breading. She went off into the bush for hours each week, gathering the herbs and roots she needed for it. The chilies, she crossbred and grew in pots behind Jim's shed.

The most popular time of the week was Tuesdays from noon to dark. It was the Shake 'n' Spear's Mystery Spear Day. Every hour Jim would combine a fresh batch of fish, turtle and vegetables nuggets, prepare them as usual and fry them to golden perfection.

Those who wanted to join in wrote down the type of fish, the type turtle and veggie on a piece of paper, and each hour Tessie would collect the entries, and Jim announced the winning trio. All who guessed right got their Shake 'n' Spear dinner free.

Needless to say, there wasn't much excitement ever going on Mahboo Island, and you can believe Mystery Spear Tuesdays at Jim and Tessie's was highly popular!

The year before, a cruise ship made four stops at the far side of Mahboo, and earlier this year, one of the cruise-line vice presidents made a visit to Jim and wanted to create a Shake 'n' Spear Mystery

Spear Excursion from their future cruises to Mahboo and make the islanders rich.

Over the years, as they sat on the beach, Jim would tell Tessie about his old world, the one where a famed British poet had dominated the literary scene for centuries and had the name Shakespeare. Tessie thought this was very funny and laughed loudly every time Jim told it. Tessie made the Shake; Jim cooked it all, and all their customers did the Spearin'.

Jim, Tessie and all their friends took great delight in telling cruise-line vice president they didn't want to become an excursion stop.

"No, thanks, this is how we like it!"

# A MODEST PROPOSAL FOR THE LAME, THE HALT & OTHERS

*Do you dare do it?*

It seems many people entertain only carefully selected people to their highly exclusive dinner parties all year long. And, some tend to defend their oft-times hurtful selections by trying to make it up at Thanksgiving.

This holiday, for such high-winding celebrationists, is their day of seeking atonement, their day to go out and bring in all the lackluster people they avoided all year, the community's lame and halt, and for them they slave, or have others slave, over a wide selection of traditional traditionals—a large turkey roasted numerous ways, endless dressing concoctions, family-original gravies, wide versions of casseroled vegetables, highly-populated whipped potatoes followed by endless pies topped with an assortment of toppings. So labor intensive; so quickly consumed!

WAIT UP. LET'S TAKE AT LOOK AT TRADITION!

Will the patriots, pilgrims and ancient ancestors come down and smite us if we happily avoid the above ritual?

Hardly!

Here is a suggested, toned-down, proposed menu for good friends, wildly popular or not—just good friends you thoroughly enjoy all year long:

NEW THANKSGIVING MENU

Fresh, crisp crudités with one or more dips

Roast turkey-breast sandwiches with trimmings:
Kaiser rolls and butter
Fresh, sliced tomatoes

Crisp lettuce leaves
Large condiment and relish platter of large and small pickles, olives, anchovies, capers, harissa, hot chilies, guacamole, cranberry relish and several sandwich spreads

Homemade Pumpkin Pie

Coffee, Iced Tea, Wine

Dare you start it?

# MACKEREL CASTLE FOR THE GOOD TIMES

## *Does a heart good!*

Old man Lothrup, they called him Doc, was a geneticist concerned with people all his career life. Once he retired, he built a castle on an unclaimed island in the middle of Lake Marigold. He then turned his biological expertise to developing a new species of mackerel, and he made a lot of headway. He took many years to breed what he wanted and kept his mackerel in a twelve-foot-wide and twenty-six-feet deep moat, which circled his castle. Just before his death, Doc signed over his island

and its castle to the Lake Marigold Heart Institute. There it stood for years, not a convenient location for a clinic or hospital.

Finally, the Institute made a deal with the city, which turned the castle into a restaurant the people named "Mackerel Castle." This meant the city also went into the ferry business to move the diners from behind the railroad station in town to the Castle's tiny wharf.

Every family spending a day at the Castle was issued a fish pole and a bucket. Once on the island, up by the moat, one member of each group fished while others read or merely sunned. The fish usually bit quite quickly, and no family left without a big, plump mackerel. Next, families were off to the Castle kitchen, with its fine aromas and marvelous organization.

Each mature mackerel, correctly named "Blue Lovely," weighed close to four pounds and was roundly plump like koi. Their fins were dark maroon, their eyes bright yellow. The bottoms of their bellies were a bright silver white, a stark contrast to the electric blue of their upper bodies. Doc had bred them for soft mouths, so they would catch easily, and he even designed a specially-shaped fishhook, which grabbed their sensitive mouths firmly.

The Lovelies tasted exactly like lobster. Trained cooks skinned them in a flash then steamed their headless, tailless bodies in specially-designed steamers for a specific amount of time. Once removed, they flaked the pure-white, tender meat onto special, wide-lipped platters, removing the entire spine. The fish meat was always served with the same simple sauce: melted, unsalted dairy butter, fresh lime juice, a touch of garlic and a tad of sweet corn juice.

A family serving of mackerel, by itself, was called the "Aziz." If they wanted serving bowls of house salad, veggies, potatoes and desserts, it became an "Aziz-Plus." A cash beer bar served drinks.

Once families collected their huge trays, they went topside to the Castle's roof, where large, planked tables afforded a splendid view of the mainland.

Roving between the tables of families eating their Azizs or Aziz-Pluses were jugglers, acrobats, moko jumbies, magicians and a team of eight specially-bred docile, drooling Great Danes meant for petting and scarfing up scraps. These were accompanied by a quartet of accordion players playing German drinking songs.

Once finished, dutiful families stacked their trays on waiting dumbwaiters and were encouraged to join in on free skeet shooting at the north end of the Castle's rooftop. Nearby a small bar served free shots of frozen Jagermeister.

At the end of the day, ferries left every fifteen minutes; families got off, went to their cars filled with delicious food, partied sufficiently and ready for a good night's rest.

The Castle was always a good deal—$100.00 per family; all had fun and a delicious meal, and *it had a heart*. Sixty-dollars from each family's ticket went to the Marigold Lake Free Heart Institute, where everybody also *"had heart!"*

# MISS PETTIS'S MIRACLE

*Patience makes Butter*

Do you remember kindergarten when your teacher may have gathered you and your classmates around her? Remember when she had you sit on mats, not far from her knobby knees?

All of us looked up, in my case, at Miss Pettis, who announced we were going to make something very special! Next to her we saw a glass bowl, a small carton of heavy cream and an eggbeater.

"Today, we are going to make our own butter," Miss Pettis announced. "Butter is an ancient food from five thousand years ago. In fact, the early Hindus used butter as we use money today..."

This brought squeals of grossness from us as we shook our hands and let out several "Eeeeeeeuuuuuuuuuuuus!"

"It was valuable," she defended, not willing to get into wallets, change purses and the like.

The class quieted down quickly, eager to see how Miss Pettis would turn cream into money.

Miss Pettis stood to put an apron on; then she put the bowl on her lap. Next, she opened the cream carton and carefully emptied all of it into the bowl. Then she began to mix the cream with her egg-beater. She confidently turned the little handle, steadily beating.

And beating.

And beating.

And beating.

Then, finally, she wasn't beating a liquid any longer! Then it got thicker and thicker.

At last, arms tired, Miss Pettis stopped beating, carefully removed the eggbeater and lowered the bowl for eager us to see better.

"The cream is all gone," some said.

"The almost clear liquid you see in the bowl is buttermilk," she said. "It doesn't look like the buttermilk we buy in a larger carton in the market. That is cultured buttermilk made from fermented milk with lactic acid. This, we have here, is traditional buttermilk."

Next, Miss Pettis handed out a flat, wooden Hoodsie spoon and a saltine cracker to each child. She then passed the bowl of our fresh-made butter among us, and each of us awkwardly put a blob of the homemade butter onto our crackers.

The children in Miss Pettis's kindergarten class thought their crackers and the brand-new butter were the most delicious things they had ever eaten.

And they never cornered Miss Pettis and had her explain how ooey-gooey butter could be used as money, carried in wallets and slipped into change purses.

# WATER'S EDGE DUCK AND QUACK CLUB

*"Jes' protectin' our women..."*

The Loyal Brotherhood of Pure Muscovys of the Water's Edge Duck and Quack Club draws a fine line between not being Barbary Ducks, intended for roasting or being wild, and being fearsome, feral Muscovy Ducks.

The peculiar wild, not-so-wild, survival game in sunny Florida gets a little complicated with its essentially filled-in swamps, random sinkholes and unexpected people/critter confrontations. One such complication is the feral Muscovy ducks of Mexican origin, usually ferocious, frequently scary and generally fearsome.

Typically, the nonferal—the good—Muscovys, laze on condo balconies and roof overhangs. The males, twice as large as the females, flaunt curious, abundant red face flesh attached to irregular, lumpy black masklike configurations—no two look alike. Their duckish cavorting lets them display ample aggression, courtship and stealth. This is reinforced by pronounced head bobbing, intense tail fluttering, rippling of crests, curious cackles and vicious hissing. On land, they dine on roots, seeds and stems of plants; on water, they chase vertebrates and crustaceans into the water shallows.

The Water's Edge Duck and Quack Club serves a noble function. Besides instilling pride in their semi-free, yet slightly domesticated, nonferal incarnation, they make it their duty to protect all nonferals from general malfunctions, which occur from time to time in their lake-o-sphere. This lake, aka Lake Alice, called by some a retention or street-drainage pond, is most Florida-necessary and what initially makes Florida so attractive to would-be residents. Add some palms, some ducks and voila—drained roads, aka sexy, glamorous Florida!

Shorebirds, and muscovys in particular, feel fortunate to dwell around Lake Alice. Their domain, really an L-shaped shore, is the north and west shores of the lake. It starts in the northeast corner of the lake next to a local Burger King. Yes, some foolish egrets get suckered in on French fry handouts from thoughtless drive-through customers. The ecologically, inside-city, out-and-out mangrove rookery, is the birthplace for most of Lake Alice's verdant shorebird population. It is spookily positioned behind an unloved strip shopping center. The rookery ends at the northwest corner of the lake, and on the west shore rests an aging condo, populated mostly by retired Florida old farts, some of whom enjoy the feathered friends and others who fuss:

"They shit, you know, and it's slippery. It makes it easy to fall down. Hate those buzzards," they love to say.

Dead center of the west shore is the condo's gazebo, the southeast piling of which is the meeting place of the Non-Feral Duck Preservation Society, WEDPS, with Bailey as its life-long president. This one corner is the exclusive territory of the unferal Muscovys. Nearby, courteous, respectful, magnificent great blue herons preen, cormorants pose, coots and gallinules nudge, the low-flying skimmers skim and the diminishing snowy egrets listen while a sharply-increasing population of wood storks confer.

All compete for survival amongst the other shore-line dwellers, the huge turtles, skittering lizards, playful otters, always-hungry alligators and huge, very elderly, large-mouth bass.

The entire Muscovy community was struggling to recover from their Ethel's recent ordeal. She is a favorite of the pure Muscovys, still good-looking, laying her share of the tribe's fine eggs when she was unmercifully raped by Igor, the feral under the gnarled fig tree, as old condo farts looked on uselessly protesting, others laughing uncontrollably. Igor thrashed Ethel, drew blood, drove her head into the dirt, hissed, growled and snorted. Feathers flew. For a moment, Ethel seemed dead, which made Igor pummel her more. At last Ethel came to, shook all over and ran away as an old fart landed a feeble blow on Igor's wing, which happily crippled it. Despite this, tough Igor managed to take to the air and flew off toward the Gulf.

Instead of eight to sixteen white eggs, Ethel's rape resulted in twenty-six eggs from Igor. They were an ugly brown with a coarse surface. Instead of hatching in thirty-five days, poor Ethel sat for sixty agonizing days, until some of her male friends decided it was time to "lend a hand." They did this by cracking them slightly to "get the show on the road." They had been accompanying Ethel once a day when she left the nest to eat, bathe and stretch. Their whole brotherhood had been on edge during Ethel's difficult nesting. Ethel was exhausted.

Out of the twenty-six Igor eggs, Ethel had a mess on her hands, and only seven chicks survived. All were relieved to realize these seven "took after Ethel."

Ethel had not been the first feral casualty. Hilda, before her, had been less fortunate—if Ethel could be considered fortunate. A memorial to Hilda was first on the agenda at the Brotherhood's June meeting. Hers was an "in-lake nailing" by Errol, the feral. Worse yet, one of the largest turtles dragged her limp body away and finished her off on the far shore.

At Hilda's memorial, President Bailey asked for a moment of silence:

"Let's be thankful that our sister, Ethel, is still with us, and let's hope as a brotherhood, we can be more vigilant against more attacks on our females."

All attending shook their tail feathers and rippled their head flesh in agreement.

"Tell you what. I propose we have all earned an outing, a feasting picnic. I propose a field trip this Saturday, 'bout noon. Those of us who are not sitting or assisting, let's meet here and go up to the parking lot, raise a little hell with the old farts and feast on the June beetle white grubs clustered around that big cottonwood in the middle, there. I checked them out earlier today, and they're beauties, a good year—and high season for them."

This brought a rousing rustling of feathers, cackling murmurs, spirited rising on haunches.

Life would be better, they just knew it!

# TONY THE TIGER RECEIVES THE BREATH OF LIFE

*Explode it, and they will eat it.*

Near the end of the nineteenth century food scientists were starting to see the revolutionary relationship between "wholesomeness" and "healthfulness."

They were learning a certain type of eating could bring about a certain result. *"You are what you eat!"* they heard. Recipes for Creamed Peas in Biscuit Baskets featured the new Shredded Wheat or "wheat pillow." A C. W. Post introduced his hot cereal-based drink, Postum, also his Post Toasties and later Grape-Nuts. The public's desire for quick, processed foods was catered to by processors such as Libby's, Armour, Van Camp, Borden and Heinz with their canned meats, soda pop, minute tapioca and canned condensed soup.

The location for the beginning of these awakenings was Michigan and its Battle Creek area, where the Seventh Day Adventists created their Battle Creek Sanitarium. On its staff was Dr. John Harvey Kellogg, as well as his wife, Ella Eaton Kellogg. They seized the opportunity to apply good nutrition along with pure living to bring about healthy results. Dr. Kellogg, referring to his wife, readily acknowledged, "Without the help derived by this fertile incubator of ideas, the great food industry of Battle Creek would never have existed. They are all a direct or indirect outgrowth of Mrs. Kellogg's experimental kitchen, established in the fall of 1883."

Born in 1853, in Alfred Center, New York, Ella Kellogg was the youngest graduate of Alfred College in 1872. After this, Ella's sister was stricken with typhoid fever, and Ella, a nurse, brought her to Battle Creek for treatment. She met Dr. Kellogg; she impressed him, and he invited her to join his staff as a charter member of his new School of Hygiene. She soon became a dietician, writer, advocate for children and social reformer. Devoted working partners, Ella and John never consummated their marriage and lived in separate quarters. However, they did raise forty children as their own, founding the Haskell Home for Orphans in Battle Creek. The couple ran kindergartens, supervised children's play and development and conducted classes for area mothers and foster mothers.

Ella Eaton Kellogg founded and was dietitian at the School of Home Economics and the School of Cooking for the Battle Creek Sanitarium. She created a new field, which came to be known as dietetics, or what she termed, "the hygiene of cooking." Much later, she and colleague Lenna Cooper, a director of training at the school, triggered the formation of the American Dietetic Association in 1917.

Kellogg's major work, published in 1892, was titled *Science in the Kitchen: A Scientific Treatise on Food Substances and Their Dietetic Properties Together with a Practical Explanation of the Principles of Healthful Cookery and a Large Number of Original, Palatable and Wholesome Recipes.*

In the book, she states, "There is no department of human activity where applied science offers greater advantages than in that of cookery." What she hoped most to get across was her belief, "The brain and other organs of the body are affected by the quality of the blood which nourishes them, and since the blood is made of the food eaten, it follows that the use of poor food will result in poor blood, poor muscles, poor brains and poor bodies, incapable of first-class work in any capacity." She also condemned condiments as "irritants, not worth the fleeting pleasure they may provide to the palate." She presented an argument against the safety of meat in a time before federal meat standards.

All her life, Ella Kellogg was extremely energetic. In addition to her day-to-day work, she formulated dietetic courses for nurses, founded the School of Domestic Economy and was assistant editor of *Good Health Magazine* from 1877 to 1920, which she published with her husband. Her column, Science in the Household ran for many years. She also wrote other books: *Studies in Character Building* (1905), *The Good Health Birthday Book: A Health Thought for Each Day* (1907) *and Everyday Dishes and Every-Day Work* (1900). She was also founder and activist in many country-wide organizations.

In 1920, toward the end of Ella Kellogg's life, she lost her hearing. To her remarkable credit, however, she learned lipreading and moderation of her own speech so successfully that few realized she had this handicap. She was inducted into the Michigan Women's Hall of Fame in 1999.

Her work companion and husband, Dr. Kellogg, (1842–1943) was born in Tyrone, Michigan. He was a charismatic, convincing charmer who thrived on the attention of others and published many works. He moved to Battle Creek at an early age, graduated from Michigan State Normal School and the New York University Medical School by 1875. He was a great admirer of the Seventh Day Adventists' movement and their approach to medicine.

The Western Health Reform Institute, world headquarters of the Seventh Day Adventists, was Battle Creek, Michigan. The Adventists avoid coffee, tea, tobacco and meat countering with more bread, fruit, vegetables and vigorous exercise. Kellogg referred to the sanitarium as a hospital, spa and boarding house "where people [would] learn to stay well." Sexual intercourse was deemed unhealthy. Some of his inmates were overweight and overworked and candidates for rehabilitation from "Americanitis." Kellogg treated these patients with rest, water therapies, room service and wheelchair socials. He referred to his regimen as "biologic living." Seriously-ill patients were not admitted. He also used this as an opportunity to foster his beliefs that sexual intercourse and masturbation were bad for one's health. He wrote much on the evils of self-abuse.

Later known as the Kellogg Sanitarium, the institution played large role in establishing the American breakfast and making Battle Creek the international Cereal City. During this time, the doctor constantly experimented with whole-grain foods and in 1890 was credited with perfecting peanut butter, a useful protein for people with no teeth. Not long afterward, John and the facility developed money problems, the sanitarium burned to the ground and the doctor fell out of grace with the Adventists, and he severed ties with them.

During this mostly successful time for John, his brother William "Will" K. Kellogg (1860–1951), eight years his junior, a sixth-grade dropout, performed mundane tasks for twenty-six years aiding his brother, the doctor. However, he also experimented with grains in a search for new cold cereals. Almost by accident, he stumbled upon a flaked mixture, which, once processed, dried and served with milk, was an instant hit with the patients. By then, his weakened doctor brother agreed to become part of Will's new Battle Creek Toasted Corn Flake Company. Later, when John was out of the country, Will bought up John's stock and renamed the company Kellogg Co. Cornflakes were then known for their great taste rather than their health benefits. Will Kellogg found he was an innovative merchandiser, and he became widely successful in the new cold-cereal world.

By the late '20s several billion bowls of cereal were sold to Americans, far surpassing hot cereals. These opened up new avenues in merchandising—prizes in packages, boxes with cartoons, puzzles, cutouts and chances to enter sponsored contests for prizes. Sugar and other additives crept into the cereals. Advertising brought pretty girls and baby contests. By this time, there were forty cereal companies in Battle Creek, and Kellogg was the most successful.

In 1925, Will Kellogg established the Fellowship Corporation, one of the country's largest philanthropic institutions. In 1930 he renamed the Corporation the W. K. Kellogg Foundation, and it has given away billions of dollars to improve the quality of life with grants and scholarships for thousands of people.

It is still active today.

# PICNIC, FLIGHT #217

## *Making up for lost time*

Their vacation trip to San Francisco, celebrating the Molinas' twenty-fifth wedding anniversary, had been cut from one week to four short days. However, the Molina family, Ricardo and his wife, Ana, and their teenage children, Alex and Christina, were determined to make the best of it.

It occurred to Ana she could prepare a special picnic for the family to enjoy during their long flight from Miami to San Francisco. A Cuban feast! They had four hours to enjoy it! What a delicious way to travel!

"I'll make Boliche! Yes, Boliche, lots of tostones, yuca, beans and rice. And, for dessert, I'll make some of my coconut rice pudding!"

Ana was very proud of her Boliche. For the trip, she would increase the ratio of chorizo sausage, ham and bacon to her eye-of-round beef. She'd make not one but three tunnels for her stuffing, a delicious one made with fresh tomatoes, green Spanish olives, lots of garlic, lots of saffron, sour orange juice, herbs, nutmeg and sherry wine. She would preslice it at the house.

Ana fried her plantains for tostones, and then she mashed them and fried them again. She also prepared yuca and a delicious salsa of olive oil, garlic, onion, cilantro and fresh lime juice.

Ana's Frijoles Negros y Arroz, Amarillo Cubano style, her family's favorite, contained raw onions, tart vinegar, crunchy cilantro and oregano over bright annatto-yellow rice topped with bright red sweet peppers.

Her Arroz con Leche pudding was her specialty— a rich combination of rice, several creams, vanilla bean, lemon, crystallized ginger, raisins and fresh coconut.

"Ricardo," Ana said, "I want you and Alex to shop for a warmer to keep the food hot. Maybe, we will need two. And, Christina, you'll be off from school the day before we leave. I want you to help me cook."

Nobody seemed to mind their assignments—a good vacation was worth it!

The guys went to several stores and finally brought home two Picnic Plus hot and cold food totes. They would each carry one onto the plane.

The big day arrived, and shortly after noon, they were seated, four across, three together with Alex across the aisle from his dad. His seat companions were two businessmen, busy with their computers.

After the plane had been airborne for almost an hour, Ana looked at her husband and raised and lowered her eyebrows a couple of times, a faint smile on her lips. It was time. They were all very hungry.

Ricardo had labeled the first carrier, "setup," and it held the silverware, plates, serving spoon and napkins. The second container held all the warm food.

According to plan, Alex rose from his seat, opened the compartment above and handed the setup bag to his sister across the aisle by the window. Christina then unloaded four plates and the serving spoon onto Ana's tray and tucked the silverware and napkins down by her side. Alex took the bag back from his sister and returned it to the compartment above.

Next, Alex handed the carrier of warm foods to his sister. Christina opened it and held each serving dish for her mother to lovingly spoon generous helpings onto each plate. She and Ricardo each held two full plates until Christina returned the second bag to Alex, and he returned to his seat across the aisle. Mrs. Molina then handed a mounded plate to Christina, and Mr. Molina handed his extra plate across to Alex.

The cabin was smelling quite good by this time, really very, very spicy, with a hearty aroma of juicy chorizo and beef, pungent garlic, aromatic onions—just an all 'round restaurant aroma—four heaping plates of it!

One attendant walked by and cheerily said, "Smells awfully good!"

Ana beamed!

Alex looked down and kept eating.

The businessman next to Alex stopped working and stared at Alex's plate.

Ana leaned past her husband and asked Alex if he'd like more yuca.

Alex put his head down and shook it. "No."

Ana was disappointed. Alex usually had three and four helpings of her special yuca.

The old lady, on the aisle behind Ricardo, stopped the next attendant and told her there was a very bad odor in the cabin.

The attendant replied, "Well, I think the family in front of you is eating their dinner."

"Well, it smells terrible. It's making me sick."

"What can I do for you?" asked the attendant.

"Make them stop eating," she demanded.

"There is nothing I can do," she replied.

The older man next to the old lady, the one behind Ana, offered, "Smells great to me!"

Ana smiled and knew they were off on a wonderful vacation.

# THE BAREFOOT CONTESSA DOES WEAR SHOES

## *"Keeping the Hydrangeas Short"*

When the world gets edgy, the news gets scary and decisions don't turn out very well, it's great to tune out reality and hone in on the abundant, delicious world of Ina Gartner, the Barefoot Contessa. Her world is so stable, so plentiful, and all her outcomes are so delicious. Her domain is a place where no one worries about calories—about cholesterol, about health, about nutrition—it's all about how to make pure, scrumptious calories even more delicious.

Just as there is a cult-following for Harry Potter—flying broomsticks, dueling, secret places and predictable sequences—the wonderful, buttery rewards in the Contessa's delicious world have their predictabilities too.

Always welcoming is the Contessa's large, shingled, rambling, weathered, brightly-lit beachside home in the fashionable Hamptons. It always allows brilliant sunshine into her busy TV kitchen where she shares her prepared menus. Her stageside stove and her super-chef's stove behind her are a symphony of silvery chrome, black, white, crystal and muted tones of butcher-block. She loves lots of salt, slashing fragrant herbs, zestily zesting citrus and "cook-testing" her cocktail shaker contents.

Her just-outside-the-door herb-and-flower gardens yield most every needed ingredient from tarragon and thyme to flowers and ferns. The Contessa has a penchant for centerpieces of looming hydrangeas with medium stems in sleek, tony crystal cylinders (medium height to preserve dinner conversation). Her table linens and dishes are predictably casual and always swanky.

Fans of the BC never know where she will serve the day's cookings, for she has many dining venues to choose from. It might be on the beach, beachfront at the house, living room, dining room, sometimes fireside, kitchen or catered at "their place." We always get to meet her guests, who seem to be live, nonactors—adoring long-standing, family friends with enamoring children who are genuinely eager to dine on her offerings.

The Contessa's husband, her beloved Jeffrey, appears to be a weekday business-world warrior returning triumphantly Friday evenings, hotel-calloused, devoted, gone all week humping for the considerable do-re-me it takes to run the Hampton manse. And every week he tends to want lowly chicken on these special evenings—chicken and Ina! Each week's chicken creation is usually a highly-caloric creation with simple vegetables, an exotic dessert and sparkling, picture-perfect, fresh-fruit-laden potent cocktails. Later, it might be mousse and a special liquor. They do all this in front of the fireplace.

Ina not only cooks during each episode, she has titles and themes for each, like the time Jeffrey couldn't spend the day with her, because he had to put in some hard home desk time. Got it—the title—"See if Jeffrey Can Remember our Courting Days" forty years earlier. As we cook with Ina, we learn about their early romantic shoe boxes of brownies and a certain eggplant dish in Paris. She has decided to make these dishes for him and see how much he recalls from those good old days. Somehow, we're pretty sure Jeffrey won't flunk. Her famous, historical brownies, we learn, are rich ones, ones calling for a full pound of butter, a full pound of chocolate, a half-dozen eggs and her signature "good vanilla."

When the BC's script timing permits, the Contessa packs us up in her snappy convertible and motors us through the quaint Hampton streets to her sample-urging cheese merchant, her amiable butcher, her desperate-to-please baker, her wine-savvy spirits vendor, her weathered fish monger or maybe her fertile-Hampton-soil farm stand.

If one consults Garten's Food Network bio, we learn her show doesn't differ too much from her real life. It seems she was a disenchanted White House think tank person when she and Jeffrey decided to purchase a tiny specialty food store in the Hamptons, which in over twenty years she grew to a large catering food emporium she named The Barefoot Contessa. She also began publishing many cookbooks before she sold The Contessa in 2003. In 2006, she and a partner went on to start a Barefoot Contessa Pantry product line as she wrote columns for *Martha Stewart Living, O, the Oprah Magazine* and *House Beautiful*.

Now she continues as a cooking host on the Food Network's *Barefoot Contessa*. Jeffrey, we learn, is a professor at the Yale School of Management. We didn't ask the Contessa her objectives, but we feel she'd say something to this effect:

"Everyone's talking low-calorie. We're talking old-fashioned, yummy rich and delicious—cooking with a taste dividend!

"How easy is that?"

# BIPEDALISM COMES OF AGE

## Visits with Mom

At first, it was very difficult for the newly bipedal to "come out." First of all, it meant literally seeming to slight those you loved who weren't able or never planned to become two-legged, a huge physical undertaking.

But, the prospect of sudden two-leggedness, being tall, seeing more, reaching higher, climbing better, throwing spears further, having hands to use full-time and actually speaking eye-to-eye, with other newly erects was, to Rectus, unspeakably promising.

Some newbies discovered they were taller than people they had known all their lives, not awfully important, but something they might have never known. Most of the men were taller than the women everyone learned. Some men even felt their children respected them more and minded them better when they were taller. So did their wives, and they began to appreciate the larger variety of games they were bringing back from further away.

Walking on two back legs freed up the arms and allowed newbies to collect large quantities of food, reach higher fruit and carry more back to the family and to share with others. It was also lots cooler moving about upright. All newbies especially enjoyed walking out into lakes further, but when it came to running, they had to admit, running on all-fours was faster. No matter. All newbies liked what they felt the future held for them.

All this caused a rift between Rectus and his mother.

"It's awful," she complained to him. "You are way up there, and I am down here," she complained. "I like to look into your face when we talk."

Recky loved his mother very much, and he knew very well her thinking on the topic. She was not impressed with his new freedoms. She even suspected he enjoyed looking down on her and other non-newbies.

Recky was wise enough not to wish for sympathy for his daily sore muscles, his throbbing hips, and his intense backaches, which started every afternoon.

Some days, he'd rest everything and attempt no uprightness. Happily, these days were becoming fewer and further between. The record for continuous bipedal among the people he knew was forty-two straight days. He knew he had a ways to go.

"Mom. I promise, this weekend I'll drop down, visit with you, even groom your lower back. How's that?" It always relaxed her and put her in a good mood.

She smiled faintly. Rectus had always been a good boy, and she was proud of him. She would never become bipedal, certainly not at her age. The friends she'd had all her life weren't planning on it, either. They were all adamant. They also had a whole lot of secret fun laughing at the those they called the "new strugglers. They knew the "bi's" were in pain but never admitted it.

She worried about Rectus being upright and making himself visible in open spaces. Being low-to-the-ground was much safer.

"Son, you have strength and youth. Me, a female, I am weaker, and certainly my years have made my legs old and unable to hold upright weight on them. As for cooling me off, you run a lot and need that. I gave up running years ago. No. I'll be down here, warmer, more protected and with my friends."

"You can keep us informed down here. We'll listen," she laughed.

# HOW I CRACK MY EGGS

## *And Other Scary Eggy Options*

There's something about an egg which demands attention. First, if you are a thinker, you puzzle why we're not *yet* warned to wash each egg, salmonella, you know! Chicken embryos are also amazing! They thicken a sauce! They whip to peaks! They make cakes and pancakes light! They bind! They turn into a salad! They cook up in ever-so-many ways!

Next, there is that thing about how to open an egg correctly. I think the correct way is how your mother did it, as is the direction toilet paper unrolls. My mother broke eggs in two with the side of the bowl, quick and simple. The Barefoot Contessa feels we should crack, not break, eggs against the countertop with a glancing miniblow to the shell, sparing its illusive membrane. Then force the halves apart. For the beginner, this can be a very drooling mess, not as difficult as for the one-handed egg jock. You've seen these jocks. With one hand only, they crack the egg on the bowl edge, separate the two halves in the one hand then allow the egg's contents to drop into a bowl. It's a neat egg performance.

Cooking an egg is a whole world of knowledge, itself:

Omelets: Do you add water or milk to scrambled eggs? Cook on high heat, medium or low? How do you get the treat in the middle?

Scrambled eggs: Egg(s), no water, no milk, into pan, break yolk immediately and stir? Let undisturbed egg rest on the heat a little, then break it around?

Fried egg: Yolk whole or broken? Yolk runny or solid? Up or over?

Poached egg: Drop into a self-generated whirlpool of water lightly laced with white vinegar? Or lower it into still water, scoop water over yolk? Done when light orange? Done when pale pink?

Soft-boiled egg: Puncture the wide end of the egg with a pin? Want the yolk to be runny? Solid and shiny orange/yellow yolk? Place into boiling water? With salt? Start with cold water? Start timing when? How long to time? Do you want to use an egg cup like the Brits? Do you want to invest in an "egg end cutter" or an egg cup? Want to prepare an Egg Spice of salt, pepper, dry mustard and cumin?

Hard-boiled egg: All of the above, but for a longer period of time, especially if you want a light, non-shiny yellow yolk. Goal—no gray halo around yolk?

What I find most troublesome is peeling a hard-boiled egg. Deviled eggs need to be smooth and shiny. Is it the age of the egg? Why is it some days, even under a running faucet, a hard-boiled egg won't peel well? It appears to be a membrane thing. A hen's egg doesn't want to peel "shell away from membrane!" Rather, after cracking the boiled egg on the countertop, roll it so it cracks all around. Now. Break into the shell and NIP THE MEMBRANE, get it under a slow, cool faucet and ease the side of your peeling thumb along the cooked egg itself, and you should get a smooth, shiny, peeled, boiled egg! Surely you devil yours with dry mustard and room-temp unsalted butter?

Another scary egg moment is separating the yolk of an egg from its liquid white. The performer's way is to crack it as you please, hopefully in near equal halves, hold them high and proceed to pour the yolk and less and less of its white from shell to shell until the yolk is clearly alone, then plunk it separately. The more secure, chicken way, is to crack the whole thing into a bowl, then fish the yolk out with a tablespoon.

Now that those egg whites are free of their yolks, they are free to do more things! Once stiffly whipped, they add new dimensions to high cakes or impressive meringues. Do they need to be at room temperature? Bowl needs to be squeaky clean? A chilled copper bowl is best? Do I add Cream of Tartar? When do I put the vanilla and sugar in?

Eggs are a handy protein; they're also demanding!

# RACE'S PLACE

## *And keepin' it that way!*

Race is a chef, a very good chef, with twenty years' experience. He excelled in Italian cuisine, yet won awards for Asian and Mexican. He feels it's fun to fuse all three.

Race's name was short for "Horace," after his banker granddad. His wife, Suzan, had a separate pastry business, and their two teenage daughters were no slouches in the kitchen. Life was good; so good, Race decided to open a restaurant. He and his sous chef, Charlie, with him for eight years, would run a popular eatery.

He and Charlie chose a wooded lot near a stream on the outskirts of town. On the property was a long-empty house with a huge deck near the short waterfall, which trickled lazily. A long driveway led to the house, one lined with huge moss-strewn trees.

Race refurbished with dull, wooden floors, which dictated a friendly, rustic theme. Tables and chairs were heavy, especially comfortable and added to the woodsy elegance, inside and out. Crisp, white tablecloths contrasted with moss-warmth tableware, and each menu item had its own specially shaped dish. Napkins were stark, elegant dull red. Stemware was rustically substantial, not tinkling crystal. It was a perfect spot to eat well in good company.

Once open, like food trucks, they tweeted "Blackboard Temptations" for the following week every Wednesday. By Friday, their next week was always booked solid!

On a particularly busy Friday evening, a middle-aged woman and her husband arrived to claim their reservation, and she told the hostess she was a food critic for the *Oakesville Citizen*. They were seated in a preassigned table.

After ordering cocktails, they settled in to study the menu, and she took a few notes. They talked very little.

"Waiter, we want to have two appetizers. I want the Jalapeno Pudding, and he will have the Aztec Chocolate Empanadas."

John was their waitperson, and he placed their order promptly.

"We'll have two more martinis, and I want more olives," she commanded next.

"No problem."

These served, the two spoke more as they got serious about their dinner order. She seemed to be telling him what he should eat, and he didn't seem happy about it.

"Waiter! We're ready."

"Please start."

"We'll start with sharing a Calamari appetizer. He wants the Caesar Salad. I want the House Special Salad."

"May I also take your dinner orders?" John asked.

She waved her hand briskly as she stated, "I want the Chili-Drenched Sole, and *he* will have the Kangaroo Meatball Tacos."

"Good choices, ma'am," John responded.

The couple's first course was uneventful.

The pair resumed very little conversation. After a reasonable time, John brought their entrees, piping hot.

The critic looked skeptically at her plate then looked back toward John, who was walking away from her. She then looked carefully in her purse, lifted a Kleenex out, waved it over her plate and then sat back as if she had never been served. Her husband quietly lifted his fork and started eating.

She caught John's eye. "Oh waiter, I have a problem. Look here. There are three black hairs across my sole, and you can see I am a blonde. That's disgusting. Take the plate, please."

John obediently took her plate. "Can I get you something else, ma'am?"

"No. I just won't eat."

Her husband kept eating and trying to ignore her.

John carried her plate directly to Race just inside the kitchen.

The *Oaksville Citizen* was a small paper in the community, and Race had been told by the hostess one of its food writers was in the house.

"This doesn't look too good," Race said.

"She's kinda high-handed," John admitted.

Race had a lot of confidence in his "Inspector General," as he called him. The inspector was Raymond, and Ray scrutinized all plates under a bright light before they left the kitchen. This had never happened before.

Confidently, Race strode to the couple's table, said he understood she did not like her meal and apologized.

"Well, you can see I am a blonde, can't you?" she said hawkishly.

"We are very sorry it happened," offered Race. "Can we do something else for you?"

"You have done enough," she said, calmly.

"We will take care of your bill," Race responded as he left their table.

Race, John and Ray met together in the kitchen, and Race announced they would just have to wait and see what happened, how far she took it. He still believed in Ray's sharp eye.

Two months went by. The *Citizen* ran no review of the new and promising Race's Place, and the whole kitchen tracked the *Citizen* carefully. They even placed a picture of the reporter/critic to the right of the Out door of the kitchen. This way they could warn Race of her return, should she try.

Finally, again, it was a Friday night, and the critic and her husband responded to the reservation they had made under another last name.

"I will wait on them myself," Race announced.

"This is going to be good," John mumbled.

144

Race smiled and walked to the critic's table. When it was time to bring their entree plates to them, Race instead invited the couple into the kitchen where he passed their plates under the bright inspection light and the "X-ray" eyes of Ray.

"No hair?" Race asked.

"No hair," the critic grumbled.

"Anything else unsavory?"

"No. I want to sit down."

Once back at their table, Race stated, "You will pick up your own check, and if necessary, I will have Jane at the *Oakesville Observer* critique your restaurant performance here two months ago."

The couple never returned. No article appeared, and this pleased Race and his entire staff.

Business kept getting better at Race's Place.

# SING ME A WAR SONG

*(Note: WWI, 1914-1918;*
*WWII 1939-1945)*

It was a time of total war; we called everything "the war effort." For the effort, we all donated materials for remanufacture for the military, and we had lots of "did withs." We *did with* very little sugar, meat, canned food, gasoline, tires, almost anything in a tube (tubes were metal then) and any electric lights whenever the sirens howled.

However, we always had our radios for our music, and it was a time when all popular music had lyrics that expressed the sentiments of everyone, grandma down to preteen. There were no groups with unusual names, no popular music concerts, no road shows, no music owned personally by musicians. Some adults owned phonographs for wax and sheet music for group sings at the family piano.

Music was written, sold and published; all musicians paid rights to use the music, and more than one artist recorded the same song. This caused greater repetition of some highly lyrical compositions and a deeper, wider number of fans.

Being sentimental about loved ones was a rampant music epidemic. All music fed to it; all listeners fed off of it—some pretty heady stuff.

War is never pretty for those who go off to it or for those left behind, and songs with their lyrics acted as soothing bonds to help bridge painful separations.

These were the "moon and June" music years, the yearnings shared; the melodies were simple. The softer the volume, the more romantic, intimate and sharing the music seemed. Hearts were heavy.

John McCormack crooned, "Keep the Home Fires Burning" and Nora Bayes belted out the assuring

"Over There, over there, send the word, send the word, over there…and we won't come back until it's over, over there."

Early recruits, sometimes called Johnnies, frequently sang songs which seemed to tell their feelings. "Pack Up Your Troubles In Your Old Kit Bag, and Smile, Smile, Smile" and "Oh! How I Hate To Get Up In the Morning." Anna Wheaton and James Harrod sang the assuring "Till The Clouds Roll By," "Good-bye Broadway, Hello France" and "It's Time For Every Boy To Be A Soldier." The Peerless Quartet countered with "We Don't Want The Bacon (What We Want Is A Piece Of The Rhine)." Dick Haymes crooned, "You'll Never Know how much I miss you, you'll never know how much I care." Bing Crosby made us feel a little worse with his "I'll Be Seeing You."

Ray Charles tried to lift our spirits when he crooned, "When The Lights Go On Again All Over The World."

Lonesome girlfriends' voices were lifted when the American Quartet pined, "Oh Johnny, oh Johnny, how you can love."

Parents' indignance was shown when Morton Harvey sang, "I Didn't Raise My Boy To Be A Soldier," and it played against Arthur Fields's "How Ya Gonna Keep 'Em Down On The Farm (After They've Seen Paree?)"

The Ink Spots rubbed it in with "Don't Get Around Much Anymore." Tommy Dorsey with Frank Sinatra and the Pied Pipers really rubbed it in with "I'll Never Smile Again" while Guy Lombardo came up with the ever-assuring, "We'll Meet Again."

To this, Jane Froman wobbled the comforting, "You'd Be So Nice To Come Home Too." Yes, it was an iffy time, and it definitely showed in the music.

The Andrews Sisters' "Drinkin' Rum And Coca-Cola" and "Don't Sit Under The Apple Tree (With Anyone Else But Me)" kept things muddling on.

There seemed to be music for every discernible yearning. On and on it went, "Far away Places," "Moonlight Becomes You" and on it went.

Just as war separates, it also fosters earlier marriages—being apart is so painful!

Thankfully, somewhere, somehow, there were a few assuring ear whisperers such as "You Belong to Me," "That Old Feeling" and the cuddly

"Embraceable You." Les Brown and Doris Day crooned, "Sentimental Journey, Gonna set my heart at ease."

As relations became more serious, so did the nation's musical drift: Benny Goodman warned, "Don't Be That Way," and Vaughn Monroe seemed to respond with "There! I've Said It Again." "I've Got My Love to Keep Me Warm," boasted Tommy Dorsey, and Hal Kemp tried to one-up him with his "Got A Date With An Angel." Ted Weems wasn't responsible for many favorites, but his "Heartaches" moved everyone. Artie Shaw had everyone wanting to be "Dancing In The Dark."

Listening also got a little worldly when Artie Shaw's Latin rendition of "Begin the Beguine," and classical with "Till The End Of Time," (lyrics set to Chopin's "Polonaise") were popularized.

Confessions of personal heartache came out in: "Full Moon and Empty Arms," the lament, "I'm Always Chasing Rainbows," "Saturday Night is the Loneliest Night Of The Week" and "Only Love Can Break Your Heart."

Lovers had heavy hearts, and those not caught up in bittersweet melancholy dealt with many at-home curtailments, neighborhood air-raid drills and too many frightened children not assured sufficiently by parents.

So, it was with little wonder that after WWII, the nation's music was filled with silly lyrics providing welcome comic relief. Many of them depicted little contrived fixes, almost anything for a laugh:

Vaughn Monroe set our imagination aloft with a ditty about "The rich Maharajah of Magador." Kay Kyser fed us some adult baby talk with "Three Little Fishies" while Kenny Roberts reminded us "I Never See Maggie Alone." When it came to predicaments, Two-Ton Baker complained: "I'm A Lonely Little Petunia (in an Onion Patch)."

We began to feel our muscle when Tex Beneke's "Hey! Ba-Ba-Re-Bop" and Frankie Laine's "Mule Train" almost gained cult status.

Maybe silliest of all was The Merry Macs' "Mairzy Doats and Dozy Doats." They later translated it to: "Mares eat oats, and does eat oats, and little lambs eat ivy, a kid would eat ivy too, wouldn't you?" It became fun to trip these words across our lips and help others do it. Another contender for word twisters was Freddy Martin's "The Hut-Sut Song"— "Hut-Sut Rawlson the rillerah and a brawla, brawla sooit." We'd do practically anything with our music to not to remember the sad tunes.

Probably wackiest of all—tunes, words and bizarre sounds—was the brainchild of Spike Jones. Most of his musical numbers were like "Cocktails for Two," which started out as a serious ballad then went downhill rapidly with cacophonies of bird whistles, portions of a kitchen band and off-tone legit instruments. These were always accompanied by hoots, hollers, whistles, screams, animal and human sounds.

We appreciated it all; we had been through a lot, and we had earned it!

# ROSEHILL REDUX

*Sometimes tourists and certain animals don't mix!*

Rex had held many jobs, from deejay to radio announcer and, more recently, a travel agent. It wasn't much fun, however, helping testy old ladies plan boring trips for themselves. Rex had written a few travel articles, as all media people do from time to time. He really wanted to work for himself and combine the two, and he had an idea.

People kept traveling to the same old places, and with the economy not so hot, travel budgets were lean.

What if new, regional destinations were promoted as more attractive?

"Almost every area has a charm or two, if well promoted," he reasoned.

The increase in bed-and-breakfast places proved this. Convention bureaus were concentrating on large groups for greater return.

This was Rex's idea: What if he developed destinations—really enhanced them, building up surrounding points of interest—and made these places attractive as new areas for a couple days' sightseeing, just enough for people to feel they had a new experience?

Rex gazed at a map and chose the town of Rosehill Pines, a short distance from an airport. It was country but not desperately remote. Rex felt Rosehill had potential.

As a Civil War buff, Rex quickly spotted a memorialized area in Rosehill Pines dedicated in 1940. It was a small, Civil War graveyard for those killed in the Great Rosehill Skirmish. He also learned someone had produced a documentary on the battle, which was on file at the local library.

The whole area was also famed for raising championship Scottish lambs and the Bah-Bah Black Sheep Chowbag Corral, which had started attracting visitors about five years ago. The restaurant, which abutted the largest county sheep farm, had a petting lamb corral for children right outside. Locals liked to eat at the Chowbag Corral mostly for their famed Bah-Bah's Pistol Hot Peppermint Double-High Lamb Chops with Scalloped Sweet Potatoes Au Gratin.

Saturday nights the "Murder for Solving" Mystery Dinner Theatre Train departed from Rosehill's little railroad station.

Nearby was the birthplace of Oliver Samuels Rosehill, an early textile manufacturer, famed for his Rosehill Clan Plaid, which was an alternative flag for local troops fighting at Rosehill's Skirmish Hill.

The original Imperial Licorice Factory still stood just east of the center of town. It was famed for foot-long purple licorice twists, which wrapped around a tiny tin-whistle prize. The factory building had been remodeled into office space, but at ground level, in one room, the Purple Licorice Museum stood. It was unmanned and had vending machine which sold Imperial Licorice memorial cards for one dollar each.

If Rosehill had its own postcard, it probably would have been a shot of their one and only lake, Lake Marigold. Cattails rimed the edges, which were scruffy. Years earlier, citizens had tried unsuccessfully to create a sand beach. This was where the cattails were missing.

Though Rosehill was a quiet town, it figured well in the state's highly-rated polo league. They even had a polo mallet shoppe across from the railroad station. Two years ago, the townsfolk built a totally new clubhouse grandstand for some rowdy viewing. Every Saturday night of the year, the Rosehill Ramblers opposed a different team at home.

On the north side Lake Marigold was Rosehill's, World's Largest Serpentorium, with some 673 residents. There were always cobras, sidewinders, bushmasters, copperheads, rattlers, cottonmouths, sea snakes and pythons. They had a staff of three snake charmers and presented snake wrestling on Sunday afternoons.

Across from the snake zoo, on the south side of Lake Marigold, was the Little Australia World Ostrich Farm and Ostrich Oasis Restaurant, featuring thirty-three ostrich entrees from Ostrich Meatloaf to Ostrich Carpaccio, even an elaborate Ostrich Mousaka on Saturday nights. The Aussies gave

Ostrich Line-Dancing Lessons while two or three ostriches themselves mingle/danced with the crowd.

On alternate Saturday evenings, the Rosehill Band Shell on the shores of Lake Marigold, diagonally-across from the railroad station in the town, held concerts. On the first and third Saturdays, the Rosehill Original Kazoo Symphony presented City Pops. On second and fourth Saturdays, Rosehill enjoyed open-mic Kookie Karaoke, and winners received valuable prizes.

Even now, Rosehill had ten potential attractions, and more would open!

Between the ostrich farm, Mackerel Castle, Waffle Wagon, Chowbag Coral, Millie's Koffee Kup, Burger-Burst, Luigi's Meatballs, Frankie's Family Eats, Molly's Muffalettas, the Stardust Bar and Grill and Polo Pappa's, Rosehill seemed to have sufficient eateries to suit Rex.

Eight B & B's, two motels out on the highway and one historical marker hotel on Lake Marigold, where Oliver Samuels Rosehill slept, seemed enough accommodations to start.

Once Rex got the owners of these places to kick into a budget toward their increased business, he would have his retainer to sustain himself while he organized some freelance writers who would place articles in papers and on blogs all over the world, and Rosehill would be on its way. The writers would be fed and bedded by participating innkeepers, the restaurateurs and the Chamber.

After Rex made a couple of trips to the region, lined out the logistics, made visits to the proposed attractions and met with the Chamber, he returned home, assembled his pitch and secured commitments from commercial participants to accommodate and feed his promotional groups, *so Rosehill could become a tourist attraction!*

When Rex presented his proposal to the mayor, he liked it, and so did the city council. The tab for Rex's services was steep, they knew, but they kept stating, "Tourists really bring in the money. We'll be opening new gift shops, more restaurants; it will put us back on our feet!" After the meeting, the mayor, the whole city council and the Chamber took Rex to dinner at the Ostrich Ranch. Rex even attempted to dance with a mingling ostrich.

Soon after Rex returned to his office and started interviewing people for his team, he received a plain envelope in the mail. It contained this clipping from the *Rosehill Ledger*:

*OSTRICH KILLS COUPLE IN RESTAURANT*

*Tuesday, May 6, Rosehill—A man and his wife keeled over, dead, onto their dinner plates as they dined at the Ostrich Oasis Ranch, at 7:30 p.m., Sunday evening. A waiter called 911 at approximately 7:35 p.m. The couple, Harvey and Jane Wallisk, residents of Rosehill, were pronounced dead at 8:45 p.m. at Rosehill Infirmary.*

*Investigators found the Wallisks died from snake poisoning while they ate, and death for both was instant. Upon further investigation, Rosehill police learned four bushmaster snakes escaped from Rosehill Serpentorium, swam the lake and attacked eleven ostriches at the Little Australia World Ostrich Farm late Saturday. Further investigation revealed the ostrich meat served to the Wallisks was a Little Australia ostrich, freshly slaughtered on the restaurant premises at 4:30 p.m., Saturday.*

*The Ostrich Oasis Ranch closed promptly at 7:45 Sunday evening until further notice.*

This unnerved Rex greatly—was it still feasible to use Rosehill, or should he develop another town?

# SHARK LADY OF EXUMA

*Rusty treasure*

There was something about little Georgetown, on the island of Great Exuma, a Bahamas out-island, back in 1992. The whole island possessed much character. Its mayor shared a sugar apple with me upon our first meeting as we sat on the wall of a small stone bridge just outside his place of business.

This was a landmark progress week for Great Exuma—UPS had commenced delivery to the island—no longer just the weekly mail boat. The islanders had a whole new way of life ahead, which none had yet totally visualized. It hadn't been twenty years since the island claimed her independence from Britain. It made one wonder when the little, young laundry worker would ever use the meticulous penmanship she was required to learn under the still-remaining, demanding UK educational system. Her former teacher, a Brit teaching abroad, lived across from our hotel. She rode the school bus to work every day as a convenience.

Our hotel, the old and famed Peace and Plenty, had so much to say just with its name. As an added bonus, Hume Cronyn was visiting as he and his late wife, Jessica Tandy, had for so many happy years. We were on a press trip starting our private plane junket with a few days on mosquito-ridden Cat Island, the guest of one of the Armbrusters and their series of curious stone cottages with attached, ceilingless, outdoor showers. Mr. Armbruster couldn't figure out why the natives built their homes up near the road and not on the beachside of their properties. A cook, a descendent of the Rolle family, made a delicious salad dressing from watermelon juice. They set a candlelit dinner for us on the narrow sand beach, almost in the lapping waves.

Very early on October 13, 1992, exactly five hundred years after Christopher Columbus "sailed the ocean blue," we flew our little plane onto the tiny island of San Salvador, recently renamed Columbus Isle. The day was hot, thankfully sans mosquitoes, and elaborate ceremonies for a couple hundred of us marked the day at the very site Mr. Columbus was supposed to have set foot on shore. Dignitaries from the Bahamian government, the Anglican Bishop and some members of the *Good Morning America* cast joined us. Just off shore, Radisson's double-hulled Radisson Diamond cruise ship anchored pristinely. We were an elite crowd!

Once released from the formalities, we made a long trek to the brand-new, soft-opened-for-us-only, Club Med, Columbus Isle. The contrast of the barren, sandy shore to this brand new, lavish, Moroccan décor was breathtaking, and it was COOL inside. The bishop blessed us, and we ate splendidly, none wanting to return to the dastardly-hot airstrip where we would head for Great Exuma.

We learned Great Exuma had no new hotels, an airport the size of a bus station and a huge reputation for offering and teaching the art of bonefish fishing. These are fish you never eat but fish you may spend a lifetime and fortune on by purchasing proper bonefishing attire, tweaking your flies and traveling to where the illusive critters hide.

As happens on every press trip, island public-relations people take writers to appropriate points of interest so they will be moved to write tempting travel stories, which will lure money-laden tourists to their shores. It was clear the island was holding a long-held breath to become a more lucrative tourist destination, and certain sites for proposed hotels were some of our visits, so were selected beaches.

Sometimes writers are treated to places they enjoy for themselves. One of these was when Mr. Rolle, our driver, another from the large Bahamian clan, brought us by "Patience House and The Shark Lady of the Exumas." Her home-museum-shop was so-named, for it belonged to Gloria Patience, shark trapper, jewelry maker and collector. We saw clippings where the self-strong, weathered woman had caught more than 1,500 sharks with just a handline, including a seventeen-foot-long monster from an old fifteen-foot Boston whaler! In short, Shark Lady's joy in life and income was finding and selling exotic seashells and shark's teeth, plus any plunder she might snag from the deep.

On each display table, Shark Lady placed little trays of cellophane envelopes. In each was a tiny, dark piece of dried, salted shark meat. She cured it, herself. At the edge of each tray was a tiny sign reading: You may not like the taste of this shark meat." This usually had the effect of most everyone taking a sample, anyhow.

Somehow, I managed to come home with a five-dollar, "antique" brass pendant, presumably from the deep, retrieved by Shark Lady. I was never into so-called antique jewelry and wasn't sure why I purchased this beaten-up looking, round pendant with possibly a one-inch bloodstone in the center. The round part had a small "handle," like a tiny skillet, which hooked onto an equally pocked, sea-beaten, booty-like, brass-like chain.

When I got home, I tucked it away, and it wasn't until much later I came across it and took kitchen scouring powder and water to it. I removed bits of barnacles, much rust, and none of it became jewelry-store-perfect. However, I did manage to bring it up to a high-mileage-looking conversational piece, one I still enjoy wearing, especially with a nice silk scarf. It has a certain patina I like.

The years have passed. The Peace and Plenty appreciates, and its role over the years will no doubt stay preserved. However, we read the Shark Lady departed at age eighty-six, yet her memory lives on. And, as Exumians so-hoped, large and luxury hotels finally arrived, a victory for their economy.

# DIVINE ABSOLUTION

## *Home Sweet Cathedral*

Lazy strands of solar refracted sunlight cleverly filtered onto Mary Beth's pale rose-granite shower walls as she eagerly disrobed, her bare toes curling into luxurious white fur carpeting. A rousing "Carmina Burana" wafted from her surrounding Bose system.

At the same time, an aroma generator noiselessly poofed into the room gentle breaths of cinnamon-vanilla-jasmine essence. Before entering, Mary Beth placed a sizeable chunk of Pierre Marcolini 97 percent bittersweet chocolate into her mouth, and it melted slowly down the back of her welcoming throat. Lit, sacred-seeming, candles rimmed the room. This was Mary Beth's daily spiritual ritual, her soul's absolution, her solace.

Her massaging Oxynator showerhead gushed luxuriating chlorine-free, oxygen-rich droplets, rejuvenating every cell of her skin and making her hair vibrant and, later, silky. The room's busy vapors enriched her welcoming lungs, bringing pure youthfulness into her entire being. For Mary Beth, this meant her body became connected to the earth and its magnetic vibrations—air, fire, water and earth vigorously enriching her throughout.

Her mantra:
I thank the great Spirit
For all I have been given
And for everything I will receive.
For all I wish for, care for or will need,
Is coming to me now, and
This I definitely believe!

During her litany, she would raise her wrists upward to catch the gentle stream of oxygenated water. This caused such relaxation that Mary Beth felt ripples of ecstasy course her entire spine.

Each of these divine times continued for close to twenty minutes. Mary Beth never failed to feel deliciously invigorated when she stepped back onto her fur carpeting and slid into her flowing double-velour tiger-print caftan. Her mind supremely relaxed, all earlier cares were released. Cleansed inside, she felt almost invincible in purpose, ready for anything.

Mary Beth was in her early fifties, and her cleansing ritual was in *sharp contrast* to her mom, who was born at the end of the greatest depression in 1930 in rural New Hampshire. It was a time before automatic washers and dryers and before scientists discovered a way to balance PH factors, bettering overly alkaline soaps which had negative effects on body hygiene. While her family had plumbing, her mom's family had no running hot water. This meant body bathing was a weekly thing, demanding many laborious heatings of water dumped into a large tub.

The last place her mom and her family sought their inspiration and general peace was family bath time. Consequently, each Sunday morning they left home for their church, seeking badly needed meditative renewal and longed-for absolution. They frequently sang this early hymn:

"There shall be showers of blessing:
This is the promise of love;
There shall be seasons refreshing,
Sent from the spirits above.

Showers of blessing,
Showers of blessing we need:
Mercy-drops round us are falling,
But for the showers we plead."

# THE EARLY GREEN-PEA MAN

*Find a need and solve it!*

We've all heard "Horatio Alger stories," where a little guy, with a humdrum life, gets fascinated by another guy's problem and invents a way to solve the guy's problem. The solver gets rich with his invention, and the problem guy gets happy.

One such Horacio Alger-type inventor was a fellow named Clarence Birdseye, and he was born in New York back in 1886. He used a friendlier name, Bob. The years passed for young Bob, but maybe he didn't study enough; for a few years later, he found himself a failing biology major at Amherst College, and he dropped out.

Bob had to do something, so he took a civil-service job as a US field naturalist, and they sent him to Labrador. In this region, freezing fresh fish happened naturally, unless protected from outdoor air, and very soon Bob became impressed with how well fish cellular structure remained when frozen rapidly. Very little crystallization occurred!

This led Birdseye to want people back in the States to experience such fish, fresh frozen at their peak of flavor and texture. He returned to New York in 1915 and developed some crude prototype equipment. He called it his "Multiplate Quick Freeze Machine." With it, he froze food in tightly-sealed cartons encased in metal. He then lowered these into a low-temperature brine solution for freezing. Later, he froze foods with calcium chloride brine chilled to -40 degrees Fahrenheit. He would use an anhydrous freezing process down the road, cutting initial freezing time from eighteen hours to ninety minutes.

You can't market perishable, frozen food without a transportation plan, especially when shipping frozen food hadn't happened yet. By 1924, Birdseye organized the General Seafood Corporation. This meant he had to develop refrigerated railroad box-cars capable of transporting frozen foods nation-wide. In five short years, Clarence Birdseye sold his company to Postum, Inc., which became the General Foods Corporation. Birdseye's line of frozen foods was renamed Birds Eye®.

Restaurants as well as businesses profited greatly from Birdseye's work. Though not the first in frozen foods, Birdseye's distinction came for his rapid process for producing tasty, well-preserved fresh fish, fruits and vegetables in retail-sized containers.

The Amherst biology dropout, Clarence Birdseye, died at age sixty-nine in 1956 in New York City. He held thirty patents and made the "Birds Eye®" name a leading frozen-food brand.

# SHUTTLE DIPLOMACY

## *Complicated jitney*

We were a motley group, slow to form, so the airport shuttle could take us to our places over in Pinellas County.

The second passenger to board was a rather wizened man, pretty obviously a dry alcoholic. His appearance was gaunt, his ears at least four inches in length, and his few teeth were far spread. It was important to him to tell us he had been sleeping on the ground with friends in the Upper Peninsula of Michigan. It was the last he spoke during our trip.

A third passenger sat on the same seat, a randy sort, the kind who "knows as much about women as he does about quantum physics." His voice, quite like a kazoo, spoke with the certain knowingness of jail cells, the raising of tough kids and several wives who hated him. He needed to be dropped where his car had been fixed at an obscure garage on Seminole Boulevard.

At another airport stop we took on a middle-aged woman, flashily-dressed, trim, rather good-looking, and she had no baggage. She sucked loudly and nervously on what sounded like an empty soda cup.

Now. The shuttle could start to deliver its people.

Not so. Our driver's dispatcher made us pick up another woman with a small cage, which held her trembling Chihuahua. She chose a seat behind the kazoo-voiced father, ex-husband and driver without a car...

The little woman with the dog was old, showed signs of earlier facial skin cancer; her hair showed evidence of home-coloring, a faded blonde. It was, however, stylishly bobbed, and atop it all was a hot-pink visor. She most certainly had been a woman of class in her time, maybe the country-club set, one people never messed with. She also snapped her chewing gum constantly.

We were a unit now, all headed to Largo. Our first stop would be to let the little woman and her dog off. We attempted to drop her at her trailer just off Ulmerton, but it didn't take. She had prevailed upon us to wait until she was inside her coach and lit her lamp. We would. One minute turned into five; five turned into ten. Finally, the driver went around to her side porch to see if she forgot to signal us. Not so.

Our driver returned to the shuttle with the pink lady and no dog cage. Her house key was packed too deeply for her to dig for, she announced. Would we please drop her by a friend's trailer a mile away in the park? We did. This time it took. She stayed. We proceeded on.

Soon we were inching along Seminole Boulevard, trying not to miss the darkened mom-and-pop garage, which presumably had fixed the kazoo-voiced man's car. He had his key out for several minutes. We found it.

"That's my '72 Chevy, runs like a top when it's not broke." He had every belief it was running perfect-ly. He got out eagerly.

Next we dropped the man with the four-inch ears at a nondescript apartment building.

Then the damsel-type woman started a conversation with our shuttle driver. He wanted her to be more definite about where she needed to go. She was very vague. And she continued to be vague.

"I don't think there's any such address," the driver told her.

"I know there is," she insisted.

Soon, gratefully, it was my stop, leaving only the classy, good-looking lady and the shuttle driver on board to prowl about seeking her vague destination.

Maybe our *driver* was the lady's destination?

# VIRGINIA'S WEARY WILLIE

## *Mom's hobo cake*

Weary Willie was an early hobo character, and he originated as a cartoon in 1895. He starred in nine silent movies and became a loveable circus-clown character. Some may remember Weary Willie today, thanks to a memorable clown figure Emmett Kelly performed with in the Ringling Brothers and Barnum and Bailey Circus between 1942 until 1956.

However, in our home Weary Willie was a plain, no-nonsense, white cake, and we ate it often. My mother, Virginia, was raised in a comfortable home where her folks encouraged their maid to cook and serve some of Thomas Jefferson's favorite dishes. Virginia graduated from the Women's College at Brown University with majors in English and economics. Things went well until she dropped out of Columbia's grad school and made an ill-advised marriage to a New Hampshire farmer. Quite soon, she found herself a single mom—well before it became a deliberate choice. She would raise me in a tenement, near Brown and her folks, on the east side of Providence, Rhode Island. The year was 1936. Ours was the only tenement with a copy of Tolstoy's *War and Peace* alongside a dark red copy of Agnes Jacques's, *A Russian Primer,* the *Complete Works of Elizabeth Barrett Browning, The Iliad and the Odyssey* and tons more I thought were boring.

Virginia, the first feminist I ever knew before I knew what a feminist was, was not a cake-carrying church lady. When she did bake, it was her usual Weary Willy cake, a Wellesley-inspired, Utah Alumni Club, cake recipe she no doubt picked up at Brown. She knew it by heart. It wasn't so much that Willie was delicious; it was that Willie was easy. Virginia wasn't into upside-down cakes, Lady Baltimores, tomato-soup cakes, pudding cakes or any of the "Surprise Cakes." For some reason, she never made pies. We got by on puddings and cake. For rare, fancy-occasion cakes she turned to Fannie Farmer. The majority of postdepression homes had no "Mixmasters" for whipping up high and airy cakes.

Virginia called the small cooking area off the kitchen our pantry. In this pantry, she made her Weary Willies, performing what this kid believed was magic. The magic occurred when her oven changed her soupy mixture into something bread-like I could hold in my fingers!

Virginia had some evidence we were descended from the Pillsburys, the flour Pillsburys, so it was always important we used Pillsbury Flour. Instead of using the called-for melted butter, she used her displacement method with Crisco, by placing in a measuring cup one-third cup cool water. Then she would spoon enough Crisco into the cup until the waterline rose to two-thirds cup. Dumping the water, she had an exact third cup. For leavening she used Rumford Baking Powder from nearby Rumford, where the giant baking powder can served as both water storage and billboard. Salt was always Worcester brand and granulated sugar was Domino's. Our milk was certified, unpasteurized from Fair Oaks Farm. Our big fresh eggs came from the weekly egg man, to whom my mother enjoyed serving coffee and, probably over time, pieces of

Wearie Willie topped with her latest courageously-concocted icing.

From my balancing position on the lower cupboard door, I watched the makings of these Weary Willies, and it was almost on cue, each time I'd ask her, when she reached above for the Burnett's vanilla, "What's that for?"

She's always responded, "To make it taste better."

Toward the end of our wonder-filled cake-baking days, I found I needed to sneak up, alone, onto the pantry counter, slide carefully across the edge of the sink, reach into the cupboard and swig a little of the wonderful vanilla—the stuff which made cakes taste so good.

Bitter—a bad experience!

I never again asked what vanilla did for a cake. I wonder if she noticed?

Virginia was a person of clean habits; however, it was a family thing to test a cake for doneness with a whisk broken from our dirty floor broom. Once the Willie was done, she removed it from our apartment-sized Glenwood Range and inverted it onto our wiggle-wire cake rack.

Virginia's Willies may have been basic, but her frostings at times stunned not-too-imaginative neighbors. She found the powdered, XXXX-sugar recipe easy, and it gave her a chance to vary flavors widely with lemon or orange rind, not yet called zest, sometimes combined with chocolate. These were in addition to furry coconut, the nutty Vermont maple flavor, smooth peanut butter or fruit jam flavors. Her favorite frosting was her delightfully pink fresh pomegranate frosting, a rare fruit for 1936 in North America.

Once frosted, all Willies went into our round-lidded tin cake box. Here Virginia practiced one more bit of her magic. About the second day, she'd place a piece of fresh bread into the box with the cake, and lo-and-behold, the following day, the bread was rigid and stiff with staleness, and the cake seemed to have taken on new moistness!

# I LOVE IT WHEN YOU WINESPEAK

## *How about some buzztalk?*

Tom, in his middle fifties, comfortable and confident, is a financial writer and likes his editor. He is no longer married and likes it that way. He sips his usually white wines every evening, interspersing them with a dry red now and then. He orders his same red and same whites by the case from same California vineyard and has been doing so for the last seven years. He rewards his hard work every evening with a wine buzz. He looks forward to his nightly buzzes.

June, in her early fifties, comfortable and reasonably confident, is a writer and an editor, depending upon which source she writes for. She is single and loves it. She likes her nightly reds when she knocks off writing each evening but breaks them up with some dry whites now and then. She buys supermarket wine in big bottles—less to carry. She also looks to her vino for her nightly buzz.

In their neighborhood live Fred and Ginny Hector, and they host a lot of get-togethers. They usually invited Tom and June, who know each other slightly. This night they are receiving at their downtown penthouse. Fred, a lifelong wine broker, knows his stuff and assumes everyone knows what he knows. Ginny, as their friends say privately, is a lifelong wine drinker. They both speak extremely fluent winespeak and have an annoying habit of coercing others to speak wine with them—especially if they perceive their opponents have less expertise than they. Most do. Predictably, these wine debates end with Ginny hissing at Fred, which causes a lapse from the wine topic and moves into embarrassing personal insults. Fred snarls viciously, unabashedly asserting his self-certain dominance over Ginny. Usually the fireworks end after guests gently slide their glasses onto trays and let themselves out the door.

At these get-togethers, about all Tom and June know is they and many others seem to be on the Hectors' *A* list, or was it their *B* list or a worse list? They also know the wine is always excellent, expensive stuff and very plentiful. The hors d'oeuvres are always some of the best, and they would actually look forward to these evenings, if they could carefully avoid the verbal fireworks.

This night Tom arrives before June and is welcomed as usual by Fred's highly-polished and forced, "So glad you're here; glad you could make it. Will you have something leggy, or maybe something chewy or crisp?"

"Red. I'm in a dry-red mood tonight, Fred," Tom manages.

"Splendid. Tell Sarah, over there, you want the new Bloody Saratoga Noir. You will love it."

The room is very full, the noise level moderate. It is quite warm from body heat. Tom doesn't see anyone he knows.

June arrives fifteen minutes later, and Fred welcomes her with his "Harrumph," smack on her right cheek. June does her accomplished glance-off of his dark beard, "Thank you, Fred; it's so nice to be here."

"You look like you need a bold, bold white; maybe something with a sparkle, my lady?"

June's wine mind goes totally blank, and she smiles helplessly.

Fred hastens, "Never mind. I have a brand-new champagne. It will bowl you over! Tell Jim, over there, you want an ice-chilled flute of Voot 27. You will adore it, and I want a full review from you before you leave. Hear?"

June feels doomed for the evening. Where can she practice? Actually, the Voot 27 tastes pretty good, but why did Fred ruin it for her? She'd get Tom to taste it, give her some buzz words.

"Tom, taste this. It's Voot 27, and tell me, in your best winemanship, what it tastes like; will you?"

He willingly takes a sip, raises his eyebrows, shrugs his shoulders and says,"It tastes damn good to me."

"'Damn good' won't do it, Tom. Seriously. Fred has put me on the spot; he says he wants my opinion about this 'sensational stuff' at evening's end."

"Oh. Poor you!" He takes another sip. "Well, let's see. Does it have legs; whatever that means? Does it possess harmony? Does it have a young or old aroma?" He shrugs some more. They are both masters of wine-mis-speak.

"Champagne doesn't have legs," she snaps. "Tell me about its aroma?"

"It smells like champagne to me," Tom smirks.

"Come on, I need help. Does it have astringency?"

"There's a little pucker there," Tom confesses. "It's definitely not buttery."

June feels they are getting somewhere. "What about the aftertaste? Is it oaky? How long does it last for you?

"I'd say it's crispy deep, nice and deep and doesn't last long enough." He grins.

"I'm thinking it's rather elegant while being a bit weighty."

"Hey, June, I came here to scarf up a good buzz and some great snacks. You're makin' me work."

"I'm sorry," June offers. "Fred dumped this on me—this party's all in a day's work for him."

"You can say that. Now, ask me to buzzspeak, and I can do that very, very well."

"Yes, Tom, describe for me, if you will, the beauty and intensity of your buzz this evening."

"Gosh, June, it's getting good. The tantalizing resilience of a bit of a hum circulates my being; if I'm not lighter than air, I'm sure getting there. Yes. There's also a smidgeon of superior, a superior edge—I'm lovin' it."

"I feel your drift," June returns. "My own buzz is beautiful, a melody, uplifting. I feel new energy, an upward dynamic, a rush of ecstasy!" She sways a little.

June looks very beautiful to Tom tonight.

"To hell with Fred. I want more Voot! Tom! Find Jim for me," June croons.

# HAND-HARVESTED WILD RICE

*It and beautiful wild flowers...*

Today, in North America, there are two vastly different "wild rice" stories. Here's how it happened:

According to early legend, "The Ojibwe (Oh-jib-way) Indian tribe migrated to Northern Minnesota from the St. Lawrence Seaway area in the late 1500s. Lead by a prophecy, they were told by their religious leaders, who possessed a shell-like "migi stone," that the spirit world would direct them to a place where food would be plentiful and in lakes. "Their wandering would also cease," explained Ron Libertus, PhD, professor of Indian History back in the 1980s at the University of Minnesota at Minneapolis. "They soon learned to increase their ricing areas by packing rice in mud balls and sowing them in more lakes…there's a mysticism about Minnesota lake wild rice, all thirty-two thousand acres of it," Libertus states.

The lure of most things wild stirs the imagination. What else springs from the earth, requires a hunting license and has officials declare an official season for it? Yet, it doesn't walk, run or fly? The answer is lake wild rice from Minnesota's land of 10,000 lakes! Few part-time, joint endeavors have bound the red and white man so historically and successfully.

Minnesota's hand-harvested wild rice is considered the original and finest. Cultivated, paddy-rice peoples' use of the word, "wild" is considered unjust. Paddy-cultured wild rice is tasty, much more readily available and costs less. In fact well over 90 percent of wild rice sold today is commercial, paddy-grown rice. A hybrid grain, developed mainly over the last thirty years, it is cultured in diked paddies, which are flooded and drained annually. Growers use chemical fertilizers, pesticides and mechanized combines for harvesting.

But, if you're a purist, a traditionalist, the historical romance of handcrafted, perfectly parched, original wild rice is a satisfying, adventuresome, textured experience. Cheese from Wisconsin, beef from Kansas City, apples from Washington State and 100 percent hand-harvested, native lake wild rice from Minnesota—if you care enough, you will prefer it and pay for it.

Early humans ate wild rice, deemed to be North America's only native grain, and it grows best in a small area in northern Minnesota. The rice plants grow three to ten feet high in shallow lakes. Actually a grass seed, not a rice, the Indians tabbed it rice because of its paddy-like growth culture. Lake wild rice is high in protein (14 percent) and relatively low in oil—a spontaneous crop requiring no plowing or sowing. At one point, wild rice became so popular it was threatened by extinction. This caused conservation measures. Natural wild rice is said to enhance the flavor of ducks and other game birds that feed on it.

Under the protection of Minnesota State Law and Indian reservation rules, the real lake wild rice is hand-harvested by two licensed people in a canoe. The rear passenger is the 'poler' and pushes the boat through the wild-rice beds. The other passenger, the 'knocker' or 'ricer,' uses a wooden flail or knocker in each hand to bend the rice stalks over the canoe and strike the tassels to loosen ripe kernels. This harvesting method serves two purposes: it allows some seed to fall back into the water for next year's crop, and the kernels inside the canoe provide the current year's important crop.

Swarthy, kind, sensitive, with a gold tooth here and there, Donald Bush, a Chippewa knocker, speaks in a soft, slow, friendly voice. "Poling is tougher work than knocking. When the lake is shallow and the boat is full and heavy, coming back into the landings is tough." Hazards for the ricer up front are getting painful rice beards embedded in one's ears; they're also very irritating in the throat. Active knockers don't talk a lot.

A knocker for twenty-six years and part-time school-bus driver, Bush learned his ricing skill from his father. The "sh, sh, sh, sh" sound of the rice spilling into the canoe is a Chippewa melody for great eating and needed cash for necessities.

Standard knockers, or flails, are twenty-four inches in length, some lightweight, others heavier. Lighter sticks are gentler and free mostly the riper, better-quality rice. Bush's white oak knockers are his preference; others prefer cedar, red oak, even pine.

Bush confides, "A few bad ricers soak the sacks before they take it for weighing to raise the weight and get paid more. One time a guy came to a buyer with rice to sell, and he had padded the bottom of the sack with four ducks he'd shot."

One dealer and processor stated, "One time when I was buying, I'll bet I had ricers backed up for two blocks. They waited patiently in their old cars, canoes on top, anxious to sell for the best price they can find. It's was all cash; we paid only the green. They asked what we'd pay, and if we were giving a nickel less than a buyer fifty miles down the road, they'd drive the fifty miles for the extra nickel.

"Wild rice is one of the few businesses where dealers pay as much as they can when they buy green, then sell it as cheap as possible. I have to pay enough so the ricers won't reject my offer for someone else's; then I mark it up as little as possible to keep it affordable for those who will pay the extra for genuine, hand-harvested wild rice."

The only way wild rice association members survived in the marketplace was to process the rice among themselves. There was no money for a middle man.

From canoe to your dinner plate, it takes seven days to process lake rice, and the rule of thumb is three pounds of green rice yield one pound of finished rice. First, the rice is set to cure on plastic tarps, which require wetting down and frequent turning until it is ready for the parcher. Parching dries the rice through a roasting process. Some of the things that make the rice different are how long it parches, how hot he gets it, and how much moisture is removed. Less moisture means the rice will keep longer and its cooked yield is greater. Next, it is hulled then polished. Following this, it is sent through a fan mill and on to the indent machine, which further cleans the rice, removing small pieces. Next, it goes on a conveyor to the width machine, which separates for thickness, then finally to the gravity table, which separates grains by weights. Mass bagging is next and on to packagers, who divide it into store-sized packages and label them. Finally, the rice is ready for gift stores and mail orders.

Many Indian families process their rice privately. They dance and jig on it. "My mom and dad did it," Bush recalls. "They placed a garbage can in a big hole in the ground, put the green rice in it and jigged on it wearing special moccasins. The kernels scratch up against each other. It used to take about two hours to get it right. They parched it for about a half hour or forty-five minutes in big, black kettles, moving the rice around with big paddles so it wouldn't scorch. Then they returned it to the garbage can and jigged on it some more. Next they thrashed it with a birch basket to separate the good rice kernels from the junk. For storage, they bought new sacks, kept it year-round in a locked closet then started acting stingy with it." He grins broadly. "My sister stole thirty-five pounds from my mom and dad once, and my mom hasn't forgiven her yet."

Don Fairbanks, five-sixteenths Chippewa, has a gleam in his eye as he recalls fond memories of his childhood when entire families camped near the ricing areas. The active, the elders and the children all pitched in on the gathering and processing. Now Fairbanks concentrates on mail order. "We ship a lot, but we haven't penetrated the east very much. However, we've had orders from Japan, Germany, the Philippines and Alaska." Don's quick to say, if he hasn't eaten enough of his rice, his fingernails tend to break. Then he eats more rice, and they're fine.

In sharp contrast, just a little south of Walker, at Ten Mile Lake, another ricing group held forth. It was an elite little group, a merry band of retired business persons and couples, white-rice gatherers. Composed of eight couples, they referred to themselves as The Consortium, and for them, ricing was a sport, part of their physical-fitness program. They held on to their rice, ate some and gave it as gifts.

Their spokesperson, Bill Macklin, a tongue-in-cheek type from southern Minnesota, made it perfectly clear that there are only two types of Minnesotans: those who live on Ten Mile Lake and those who wish they did. Their consortium reasoned that ricing was far more productive than fishing or hunting, "because we're always sure we'll come home with some of what we set out for."

Judy and Bill Macklin often serve guests Wild Rice Soup, reportedly served at the governor's mansion, and use the recipe taken from the *Governor's Pantry Cookbook*. Prized lake wild rice turns up in countless recipes on festive and everyday tables in compotes, salads, stir-fries, casseroles, cereal, braised with any wild game or birds, added to pancake batter, soups, stuffings and desserts. Some make pasta using part wild-rice flour with part white, unbleached flour. Professor Libertus likes his rice plain with nothing but soy sauce.

Loosely knit, extremely dedicated, the Wild Rice Association committed itself to a very tasty tradition.

They continue to keep the faith and do their best to see their hand-harvested seal doesn't turn up on paddy-grown rice packages.

Professor Libertus concludes, "So, if your grandmother in Peoria is to receive the romantic wild rice, you're going to have to pay more, because it is all hand-processed. Just like anything else, a handcrafted chair is more costly than one made on an assembly line. I tell the native growers not to worry and to continue to concentrate on marketing luxury, handcrafted rice."

The red man gathers; the white man distributes, and the faithful preserve an ancient tradition. The rice is in their blood, a gift from the land where the Native American and the white man have a rare, symbiotic relationship. Both groups are committed to not seeing lake wild rice become just another lovely roadside wildflower, something delightful to behold but no longer valuable.

2012 update: Where do true wild rice and paddy-wild rice stand today? Below is a statement by the Manoomin Council (http://www.manoomin.com/Ecology.html).

Real Wild Rice vs. Paddy Wild Rice
Many consumers confuse paddy-grown wild rice with the true wild rice, hand-harvested from northern lakes and rivers. Frequently, the wild rice offered for sale in local grocery stores or at roadside markets is paddy-grown rice—a different product than the true wild rice taken from naturally growing stands of manoomin.

Paddy-grown rice has larger, darker (almost black) kernels, takes longer to cook and lacks the distinguishing nutty flavor and fragrance found in native wild rice. Paddy rice is farmed in large rice paddies and mechanically harvested. Commercially grown, paddy wild rice comes mostly from large paddy fields in Minnesota and California.

# DEATH BY MARSHMALLOW

*"Jes' keepin' it natural…"*

After Elmer retired, he loved to fish. He spent a lot of time doing it; plus it got him away from Hilda, his wife, who despised him. He'd give most of his catches to his neighbors, because Hilda wouldn't cook them or couldn't? Elmer married poorly.

Hilda wasn't just a bad wife; she was an aggressively-bad wife. Years earlier, she had turned their two daughters against Elmer. She continually altered the groceries Elmer bought for himself, adding salt to his sugar container, leaving certain perishables out all night then returning them to the fridge early the next morning. That way Elmer fixed himself a lot of spoiled food. Earlier in the month, she put brown sugar in his truck's gas tank.

Elmer's unloving wife spent her days in the same chair in the corner of the back screen porch, turned so she could not see her husband as he fished. Some nights she slept the night in her chair, never going to her separate bedroom. She never said anything pleasant, not even on the telephone. She didn't read. She didn't watch TV.

"She only thinks about new ways to annoy me," Elmer supposed.

Elmer longed to be single, to have their Florida first-floor condo to himself, not having her nag every minute he was at home. This caused him to be out of the condo more, fishing in Lake Ainsworth just behind the condo and being in the out-of-doors he loved so much. The intense green of palms, weeping willows, huge live oaks and expansive fig trees made it very peaceful. At the same time, it was live and exciting, thanks to many large shorebirds and their bretheren—some over two feet tall—anhingas, egrets, coots, gallinules, wood storks, great blue herons, mallard and Muskogee ducks, otters, six-foot alligators and a pleasing variety of fish to delight the angler in him.

Usually, when he fished, Ainsworth Lake's alligators swam north to south, south to north, out in the center of the lake. There was something rhythmic about this, Elmer felt. It while pondering the stealthy alligators that Elmer hatched an idea. It was an idea which made Elmer increasingly happy. The more he thought upon it, the further he developed it. He was developing a plan. In his head, he called it the Hilda Relief Plan, a plan, he hoped, to relieve him of Hilda's hate-filled presence and possibly end for her what couldn't be a happy life. Could it?

It was on a Monday. Elmer started tossing one marshmallow into the lake. He threw it out quite far. Three days later, he threw three marshmallows a little way out from the shore. He repeated this every three days for the next two weeks. Next, he tossed two marshmallows only a few feet from the shore, and he did this every other day for a whole month. During all this, Elmer enjoyed his fishing each day, always tossing, on appointed days, his prescheduled marshmallows just as he finished fishing.

Elmer hid his marshmallows in his truck, under the passenger seat. It was getting to be time to draw his friends, the alligators, into his domain and get them lined out to do his bidding. After the month-long schedule, he planned to make things close and planted two marshmallows right into the shoreline mud, not fully burying them. He did this every other day for two weeks; the next two weeks, he punched his two into the soft mud every day when he left.

Elmer was getting a big nervous, but he was still excited about the plan and eager for its result.

Every day Elmer noted the alligator activity closely, and it was a fact—they were making their laps much closer to his side of the lake, not in the middle as had been their habit. He expected this. Things were working for him!

Next, Elmer started leaving three marshmallows on the shore itself, up where the ground was drier, and ACTUALLY TWELVE INCHES TOWARD THE CONDO PORCH!

He was concerned, though; he was not seeing any alligators, themselves, lurking near him as he fished, getting selfish and a bit aggressive, which hand-feeding animals in the wild does. Was his plan working or not? After dark, one night, Elmer took a small flashlight and went down to the shore. He wanted to see if the three marshmallows were disturbed and possibly see if any alligators were loitering near the shoreline.

To Elmer's alarm, he nearly stepped onto the snout of a half-beached alligator; all three marshmallows were gone! Elmer hastened back to the condo; Hilda snored as she slept in her chair. This was good! However, Elmer's close call had his heart pounding!

This knowledge, this progress, meant Elmer could step up his plan, as it seemed almost ready to work! The next night he would cut back and leave no marshmallows, and the following night, he left two a little further inland, about three feet. The next night he left none; the next night he left six about eight-feet inland. He repeated this for a week.

Now it was time for Elmer to do his in-house work. He deftly detached the lower panel of the screen door to the porch then made it look unbroken by taping it gently from the outside. He also placed four marshmallows just inside the screen door in several plant urns. That done, he would make the next night, Wednesday, attack night. In his favor, it was scheduled to be a moonless night.

About eight thirty, just before total darkness, Elmer went to the shore edge and created a path of marshmallows, one every yard, through the grass from his usual fishing spot on the shore leading straight to the broken screen of Elmer's and Hilda's Florida condo back porch.

This done, Elmer retreated into the porch, double-checked the looseness of the screen, spread some marshmallows at Hilda's feet as she slept—snoring combatively—walked through the condo, exited through the front door, got into his truck and drove upstate to visit his aged mom, a trip he made every month.

It would work, if he did everything right. "It has to," Elmer muttered.

Elmer returned home about noon on Friday, and nothing seemed unusual from the outside.

Once inside, the front of the condo looked as usual, so too the kitchen. Elmer heard nothing, no snoring, and stepped out onto the screened porch, decorated excessively in red, red from Hilda's blood. Everywhere. Ceiling. Walls. No bones. Just a whole lot of bloodstains, like Hilda exploded!

Elmer was shaken, yet very happy. He stood there, numb.

Then suddenly a brighter shade of red splattered up against the darker red on the ceiling, the walls and floor.

This is because Elmer, himself, was impaled!